SAINT RA

Michael Bracewell was born in 1... ...published
two novellas, *The Crypto-Amnesia Club* and *Missing
Margate*, and three novels, *Divine Concepts of Physical
Beauty*, *The Conclave* and *Saint Rachel*. He lives and
works in Surrey and Manchester.

BY MICHAEL BRACEWELL

Michael Bracewell

SAINT RACHEL

VINTAGE

Published by Vintage 1996

2 4 6 8 10 9 7 5 3 1

Extract from *Addition to Perfection* by Marion Woodman,
reproduced by permission of Inner City Books, Toronto;
and from *Listening to Prozac* by Peter D. Kramer
Copyright © 1993 by Peter D. Kramer.
Used by permission of Viking Penguin,
a division of Penguin Books, USA Inc.

First published in Great Britain by
Jonathan Cape Ltd, 1995

Vintage
Random House, 20 Vauxhall Bridge Road, London SW1V 2SA

Random House Australia (Pty) Limited
20 Alfred Street, Milsons Point, Sydney
New South Wales 2061, Australia

Random House New Zealand Limited
18 Poland Road, Glenfield,
Auckland 10, New Zealand

Random House South Africa (Pty) Limited
PO Box 337, Bergvlei, South Africa

Random House UK Limited Reg. No. 954009

A CIP catalogue record for this book
is available from the British Library

ISBN 0 09 946471 3

Papers used by Random House UK Ltd are natural, recy-
clable products made from wood grown in sustainable
forests. The manufacturing processes conform to
the environmental regulations of the country of origin

Printed and bound in Great Britain by
The Guernsey Press Co. Ltd., Guernsey, Channel Islands

For Nicola McAllister

'At a certain point in my life, in the late 50s, I began to feel that I was picking up problems from the people I knew. One friend was hopelessly involved with a married woman, another had confided that he was homosexual, a woman I adored was manifesting strong signs of schizophrenia. I had never felt that I had problems, because I had never specifically defined any, but now I felt that these problems of my friends were spreading themselves onto me like germs.'

Andy Warhol: The Philosophy; From A to B and Back Again

The Shrine of Saint Rachel:

Neroli	Diazepam
Nan Goldin	Prozac
'Jack the Ripper'	'Hypnotic Suggestion 505' (1993)
Red Jackie (1965)	Dan Graham
Propranolol	'The Murder Mystery' (1969)

One

The rain had not stopped all day. From first light the clouds had been low over London, the centre of the city dark and glistening as it seemed to hunch beneath the torrent. The rain fell hard in straight lines; the air in the streets was cool. In the parks and city gardens, the flowers and blossom of early April stood out in vivid disarray. Above black railings, the budding trees dripped.

Through the crowded halls of the museums and galleries, along the thronging aisles of the department stores, above the desks and the overflowing waste-paper bins of the big, open-plan offices, in trains and on buses, there hung the sweet, unhealthy smell of wet and drying clothes. The rain had dominated the day, finding its way into thought and conversations, as well as the lobbies of grand hotels and the booking halls of the underground railway stations.

Now, in the late afternoon, as the working day drew to its close and the traffic shuddered in long lines, the hordes of hurrying pedestrians made their way through the city with their heads lowered beneath umbrellas and their collars turned up. They walked more quickly than usual, and grimaced as they paused in ranks to cross the busy streets. The ceaseless rain seemed to set them apart from one another, and to raise in each an ill-tempered determination to outrun their fellows. The light, now, was the colour of amber, drawn from a pale horizon, and the gap between the raindrops was widening, but as the rain continued, as though in a different key, the sky was growing brighter. John White, standing in a doorway in the Haymarket, was aware of this shift in the light as he watched his wife going into a cinema with a man he had never seen before.

Later that evening, in a dark and noisy basement restaurant, where tall blond waiters hurried and swerved with trays of Maryland crab cakes and green salad held high, John recounted the story of his day to his cousin, Sarah. The small table at which they were sitting, tucked into a dim alcove, distanced the cousins from the rising volume of voices, the clatter and sparkle of cutlery, and the endless passage of diners, their faces indulgent or set, as they moved from the bar to their tables, or greeted one another with short barks of welcome. Sarah, sitting with her back to the wall, allowed her intelligent gaze to flick without pause over the details of this inconsequential clamour, as she listened to John. His words came in close-knit clusters, the speech of a person who has been talking to himself in his head, all day. His white raincoat was draped untidily across a chair; his suit was creased. He had lost his tie the previous day. Sarah was smart and well-groomed. Her dark suit was neatly belted, her open-necked blouse revealed healthy, well-tended skin; her small earrings and her straight brown hair, cut with a modest fringe, all contributed to her poise and alacrity as a successful businesswoman. But this countenance disguised an inner sympathy; she was sorry to see John so troubled, but she did not know what she could do to help.

Her cousin's face was pale, and his famously blue eyes were red-rimmed with fatigue; his corn-yellow hair, pushed back behind his ears, looked greasy and unkempt. His attractive laziness, which had made him humorous and charming, had been replaced by a nervousness which rendered him insubstantial. He was struggling each moment, it seemed, with sudden stabs of fear; only his jealousy and his despair were strong enough to distract him from this morbid state of self-awareness. Sarah, remembering the date of John's birthday, would remember to tell Robert, her boyfriend, that John was only thirty years old. She was nearly forty; she made more money than her cousin, even though he didn't have to work, and she believed that she enjoyed a better quality of life. She had watched people at her office, over the years, being held together by the drugs which John now had to take; panicking in the shallows of mental illness, the depressives and the neurotics had all either learned to swim or drowned through sheer exhaustion. Theirs was a looking-glass world, so cruelly similar to reality that it offered illusions of hope which only shattered when touched. It was an increasingly busy world, too; as Robert would say: 'There's a lot of it about . . .' Out of the noise of the restaurant, John's voice broke in on Sarah's thoughts.

'People,' he was saying, 'have always confided in me;

3

it's a way I have – I don't know why. Even people I hardly know will tell me about stuff that their partners don't know, about the problems they never got over and the people they nearly married. But in the one case, the one rotten case when it really mattered . . .'

Sarah's gaze returned to the busy restaurant: a theatre crowd were sitting down, opulent and confident; there was a table for two disgruntled lovers beneath a brass-shaded lamp – he patting his fingers together, and not speaking, she rising immediately to seek the cloakrooms: a fight brewing. Sarah tried to concentrate on John. Of course, the problem was Anne, if it had a name; the problem had always been Anne. She hoped that John wouldn't cry, not in public; for all her concern, Sarah would have found tears embarrassing – the outside of enough, as she put it to her friends.

To Sarah's analytical mind, which calculated the value of information as though by weight, the story of John's day was both slender and baffling. From eight o'clock in the morning, until his sighting of Anne at just after six, he had walked the same route in the rain, over and over again. Beginning outside the Royal Festival Hall, where the paving of the upper walkway was flooded beneath broad, shallow puddles, he had made his way across the cinder-coloured length of Hungerford Bridge, pausing from time to time to look down at the rain-pitted river. Behind him, the morning trains rattled and clanked into the futuristic maw of Charing Cross station; ahead, he had seen the low white arch of Waterloo Bridge, which underlined the misty towers of the City beyond. He had felt overpowered by the indifference of London towards his mission: not one detail of the view, from the grey, geometric slabs to the south, or the wedding-cake spire of St Bride's to the north, possessed any quality to remind him of any good in himself, or in unknown others. The wet morning had drained the city of sympathy. There was nothing but damp buildings and the slow irritation of busy, uncomfortable citizens.

On the steps which ran down to the entrance of Embankment station, on the northern bank of the river, John had seen spirals of fine mud in the rainwater which lay across his path; on a level with the station's low roof, he had seen fractured blue crates and a coil of rusted wire; some posters, scraped and torn, announced a Craft Fair for the homeless, to be held in a crypt. But the homeless themselves, as John walked with sudden purpose through the echoing hall of the underground railway station, to the foot of Villiers Street, were nowhere to be seen. Two Asian boys were unloading magazines; a flower-seller, the corners of his mouth drooping with distaste, was pouring himself some tea from a flask as he stood beside his laden stall. Irises, carnations, pinks, lilies and daf- fodils, their petals sparkling with moisture, had made a controlled explosion of colour against the drab mon- otony of the street. A taxi had turned the corner, splashing a young woman; its wheels had hissed on the wet road.

As John was recounting these scenes to Sarah, he realised that the whole day had remained intact in his memory; he could run through the sequence of events, and pause on selected details, as though his recollections were unedited film. And the frames of this film contained images which were both vacuous and vivid; they had achieved clarity, or significance, to John, because of the drama to which they were leading. For John, the impact of the day had occurred at its end, when he saw his estranged wife, and now the resonance of that impact was reversing to animate the banality of the whole. John's voice was first low and urgent, then a smokey drawl; he fiddled with a cigarette or a bottle-top as he was speaking. The pain which he felt at missing Anne was a physical pain, aching through his bones. With her coffee, Sarah drank whisky; she had decided to give her cousin until eleven to disburden himself. She was trying to remember where she had parked, in the anxious confusion which had thrust the mess of John's day into the order of her own. Mostly, she hated the thought that her handsome cousin might easily become a bore.

Reaching the top of Villiers Street, John had paused once more. The Strand was blocked with traffic, inching its way into Trafalgar Square. At Charing Cross station he drank decaffeinated coffee. Sitting at a white plastic table, beneath a featureless arch, he had watched people meeting one another and going about their business, their lives locked behind their eyes. The multi-coloured sugar had made circles of pink and blue in the froth on his coffee, and these he smoothed into new shapes with the back of his spoon. From time to time, gusts of rain had blown in under the arch; cars pulled in and out of the station forecourt, jolting to a halt as they tried to find a gap in the traffic. And still John sat at his plastic table, trying to watch every face, and hoping but not wanting to see Anne. He knew that Anne worked in a large office, which stood on a corner to the west or the east of Trafalgar Square. She walked, every weekday, from Waterloo to her office. John felt that he was sitting in the centre of his wife's world, and that he had violated some privacy.

'But why didn't you just ring her?' asked Sarah, interrupting when she ought to have kept silent.

'Because I couldn't . . .'

The newly-built shops which were just opening, and the corridors of damp wood which formed a pedestrian tunnel through the intricacies of scaffolding, were all, to John, custodians of his wife's independence. Even the reflections of jumpers and skirts – watery turquoise shadows – in the windows of a clothes shop, seemed to resent his presence like women defending an offended member of their sex. The morning crowds had surrounded John in his shame. He knew that he had no right to follow Anne, now that she had started her new life without him. Walking towards the covered basins of the fountains in Trafalgar Square, he saw that the working day had begun. He was adrift in sudden vastness; before him, the long low bulk of The National Gallery offered shuttered windows to the grey day. To the left of the gallery more building was in progress. Turning, John glimpsed flags and golden cord through the central portal of Admiralty Arch. A siren cut the air with its abbreviated whoop; blue lights flashed momentarily on the roof of a police car.

Sarah, recrossing her legs beneath the table, could only see the hopelessness of her cousin's situation; she was embarrassed for him, and wondered at his tenacity to the past. 'You can't go back,' she said, but John wasn't listening. She remembered the wedding in Sussex – it had been raining then, too. On a wet Saturday afternoon, five years earlier, John and Anne had stood on the broad stone steps of a church near Lancing. Everyone had been so pleased for them; it had seemed more sincere than any other wedding Sarah had attended. Anne's slight smile, almost mocking, had described the fact that she found herself amusing as a bride. In her long white dress, with its stiff gauze veil pushed carelessly over her shoulder, she had descended the church steps with extreme caution, her right arm resting lightly through John's. She had mimed a tumble, which raised a loyal laugh. Anne, who had never done anything that she didn't want to do, and whose popularity and single-mindedness had made the notion of her marrying seem somehow impossible, was a woman whom all clever men admired. She could drink more than most men, tell funnier jokes than almost anyone, mimic her detractors with ruthless accuracy; she had travelled around the world not once but three times; one of her bridesmaids was Indian, the other from New Orleans.

Anne had met John on the platform of Worthing station, one damp May morning, and they had argued about a lost umbrella. Their early romance, so Robert

8

maintained, had had the plot of a musical comedy. 'It only needs songs,' he had said, 'to star Judy Garland and Frank Sinatra . . .' Sarah recalled this quip as she noticed the nicotine stains between the first and middle fingers of John's left hand. Anne, too, had remarked that left-handed smokers were rare; but she had liked the way that John held his cigarette pushed down between the lower knuckles of his fingers. In others, the mannerism would have looked affected; in John, with his vivid blue eyes, his untidy blond hair and his striking good looks, the lazy posture of his smoking had seemed boyish and elegant. Other men, less at ease in their skins, had tried to imitate him; other men, too, had been jealous of John for his tall, pretty wife, and of the obvious friendship which had existed at the heart of their marriage. In John and Anne's marriage there had been, for three years at least, a close harmony of strength and devotion; neither partner had consciously led the dance; both had known, as if by nature, when to assert and when to withdraw, combining and respecting different aspects of themselves in order to ensure the safety of their secret world and their private laughter. Such was the constitution of their love, and their defence against the world. It had been, initially, an efficient chemistry of tremendous beauty; but, thought Sarah, there had been some cruel smiles when the chemicals had gone bad. Sipping her whisky, Sarah glanced at the collage of small, framed photographs which covered the restaurant wall: they depicted silver-haired men wearing dark glasses, drinking on Venetian balconies, or smiling into the camera beside relaxed

American girls; there were distinguished ladies, framed in Gothic arches – one feeding a sliver of carpaccio to her Sealyham – an intimate record of the Mediterranean playtime for rich Italian Americans during the nineteen fifties and sixties, their summer made eternal on black and white film. Indifferent to the present, the faces of these wealthy strangers responded to a private party beneath glass. The confidence of their expressions was secure forever. And so it had seemed for John and Anne. Sarah turned back to her cousin's voice; she couldn't tell whether or not he was drunk.

On the northern side of Trafalgar Square, shortly after half past nine in the morning, John had rested against the wet stone of the balustrade and tried to collect his thoughts. His way lay west, towards the Haymarket; the limit of his patrol would be the statue of Eros in Piccadilly. Beyond the pedestrian crossing he saw pale lights in the high windows of a private bank; beyond the bank there was a busy road junction; beyond that, then obscured by a passing bus, were the grey marble pillars and smeared glass doors of a squat office block which bore no name. He started to walk once more, slipping quickly between the wet, waiting cars as though summoned to an urgent appointment. But in his mind he had been talking to Anne. First, he apologised to his estranged wife – they were not divorced, he reminded himself – for following her to London; she listened impatiently, to begin with, and then lowered her head in sorrow.

'It doesn't matter what either of us have done, or not done,' he said, earnestly, 'the point is that we love one another, and neither of us will be happy again, or complete again, without the other . . .' Anne, shivering slightly, took his arm as she always had done; they stood beneath the dripping awning of a small coffee shop. 'I've changed,' John said, 'I've grown up and got things going – things to do . . .'

'Have you?'

'Really; I'm so busy now; you wouldn't believe it; it won't be like it was. Please Anne, come back – if only for a few days. Just see. I miss you. It's not a question of analysis . . .'

'I miss you too, John.'

The images had faded, and Anne's voice had dissolved into the noise of traffic. Looking up, John saw dour-faced tourists enduring the rain: Americans, sporting beige raincoats, were heading towards Jermyn Street; some stoical Swedes, the hoods of their anoraks laced up tight, were marching soundlessly towards Leicester Square. John looked into the colourless eyes of a young man whose hands were long and red and whose fair moustache straggled over his upper lip. When John talked to Anne in his imagination, she seemed to be incapable of the viciousness, and the decimating indifference, which she had shown to him shortly before they had parted. She was a pre-problem Anne, from when life had been healthy. Then John had seen Eros. A sign announced a flooded subway. He rephrased his imaginary plea to Anne: 'It doesn't matter what either of us might think . . .'

Sarah called for the bill. With a barely perceptible nod,

she had attracted the attention of the waiter, and made the light gesture of a signature against her palm.

'And so?' she said, looking at her cousin.

'And so I walked the same walk maybe fifteen times; or not as many as that. I stopped for a sandwich.'

'So when did you actually see Anne?'

John's expression was numb, mechanical. 'Around six; it was her, definitely, and some man.'

'Are you sure it was her? I mean, if you'd been working yourself up into a state, all day, you might just have thought . . .'

'It was her. She was wearing the coat that I bought her.' John paused, thoughtfully, as though an important detail had just occurred to him; 'She had a different bag though,' he said, 'like a briefcase.'

Sarah took a breath, but was then distracted.

'There's Ben!' she said, suddenly. Smiling broadly, she waved at a tall young man who was making his way between the busy tables.

'Sarah! We meet again!' The young man hurried over. He was powerfully built, more portly than muscular, with crisp, golden hair and a plump face. His nose was small and childlike, and his eyes were bright and friendly behind the lenses of his round, gold-framed spectacles. He was wearing a dark pin-striped suit, the buttoned jacket of which stretched loosely across his paunch. His crimson tie was pulled down beneath the open collar of his white shirt. He had the air of a man who enjoyed life to the full, who plays the part of an amicable libertine while negotiating the problems of each day with many good-natured sighs. But he was also a conscientious company man. He worked for the same firm as Sarah, and treated her, fraternally, as one of the boys. He kissed his colleague on her slightly turned cheek and nodded at John with a smile.

'I haven't seen you since that do at New Year;' he said to John, 'All well in . . .'

'Not so bad . . .' John made a dismissive gesture with his hand; 'And you?'

'Ask the boss!' Beaming, Ben rested his hands on Sarah's shoulders. Sarah had been promoted.

'Oh, shut up!' Sarah pushed Ben away with a laugh. 'What's the big party?'

Ben looked startled. 'What? Oh . . . That's some clients of Christina's and a few people from her office.'

'How is Christina?' asked Sarah, pointedly.

'Fine, fine. Only another three months before D Day . . .'

'God! Is it due that soon?' Sarah glanced at Ben's wife; 'She looks incredibly well . . .'

'Well, she was sick in the mornings, at first; but now, touch wood . . .'

There was a second of silence. 'Hey,' said Ben, urgently, 'why don't you two come over and join us for coffee? I know that Christina would love to see you . . .'

'But she's working.'

'Call that work!' Ben lowered his voice, conspiratorially; 'Between ourselves, it won't be worth the paperwork . . .'

'It's kind of you,' said Sarah, 'but we were just going. I'll see you on Monday.'

'Indeed you will . . .'

Ben extended his warm, fleshy hand to John. 'Good to see you again. Give my love to Anne. We'll drop by and see you, the next time we're in . . . Where was it? Worthing! That's right – Worthing.'

John smiled, and shook hands.

'Bye!' said Sarah, waving. She turned to her cousin. 'Sorry about that . . .'

'There's no reason why he should know; he's nice – I like him . . .'

'Ben's great.' Sarah signed the credit card slip, and handed it to the waiter. 'Where are you staying tonight?'

'The Chatham; I took a room for the week.'

Sarah shook her head, as though bemused. 'The Chatham! God, I didn't know that place was still going . . .'

John nodded.

'I don't approve of gentlemen's clubs,' she continued, 'you know that . . .'

'It's cheaper than an hotel . . .'

'I still don't approve.'

'Neither did Anne . . .'

Sarah swallowed the last of her whisky. 'Well, I'm with her on that, at least. Robert wanted to join the RAC Club – to use the swimming pool, he said. But it was just peer pressure; it wasn't Robert. It was completely out of character – signing up to a woman-hating institution . . . He didn't do it in the end . . .' She paused. 'I just feel that way,' she said, 'Sorry.'

The cousins got up from their table. John looked down at their empty glasses, crumpled napkins and half-filled ashtray. He felt that he was leaving a temporary sanctuary from the morbid thoughts which terrorised him. His three glasses of wine – he had hardly touched the third – had left a dry, metallic taste in his mouth. They pushed their way through the crowd of late diners who had gathered beside the long, dimly-lit bar; the noise in the restaurant had increased: conversations were louder, the busy waiters rushed from the tables to the kitchens, smiling less and calling out new orders to unseen chefs. The restaurant, whilst not expensive, was unadvertised and exclusive; the diners had the air of being among their own kind. The Friday night atmosphere was becoming boisterous.

As she was collecting her coat, Sarah met some more people whom she knew. She introduced her cousin, and John had the sudden sensation of two separate evenings meeting, like rowing-boats gently colliding amidst apologies and laughter. After a few minutes, he climbed the dark stairs and went to wait for Sarah on the street. The padded door swung shut behind him, cutting off the noise of the restaurant as though a radio had been turned down. The restaurant door was marked only by a street number and a muted yellow lamp. The street, running parallel to the Strand, was narrow and poorly lit. It was little more than an alley, the width of a car and a thin strip of pavement. The high, dark backs of two hotels, featureless save for the diagonal flights of fire-escapes, faced the entrance to the restaurant. At either end of the narrow street were lights and bustle; the Friday evening had brought out crowds of people, laughing and shouting as they made their way towards Covent Garden. There were scarlet lights shining cheerfully in the distance, and window reflections the colour of brightly polished brass. Loud music was playing in a bar on the corner.

Waiting for Sarah, John went over his day once more; it seemed unreal. He wanted to rouse himself, and to know that he had not seen Anne with a stranger; he wished that the new Anne, who didn't care about him anymore, was just a dream. Then John found that he resented London because it was sheltering his wife; he had never been jealous before. He longed to know who Anne's companion might be: he had only glimpsed them for a few seconds; Anne wearing her long coat, and the man a mere impression of a man, his head turning swiftly before they disappeared from view. The facts were incredible, to John, and he longed to deny them. He was jealous of the man because he admired Anne's taste; people were usually flattered by her attention. He recalled the way that Anne would twist the tiny silver butterfly on the back of her earring; it was an old habit. 'I know that you're really listening to me when you do that,' he had used to say. The restaurant door swung open.

'People!' exclaimed Sarah, pulling on her coat.

'People,' repeated John, uselessly.

Sarah squeezed her cousin's hand. She had hoped to

offer him encouragement and advice, but there were no goals to aim at and all the facts confounded hope. Anne had made her decision to live away from John, her reason being that she no longer loved him, more than a year earlier. Incapable of dishonesty and determined to free herself with room for neither false hope nor false friendship, she had made her reasoning quite clear to her husband.

'It's over. I'm leaving,' she had said, in her quiet, firm voice. She spoke more slowly than usual, and throughout her pronouncement John had run his finger up and down the spine of a magazine that was lying on the sofa beside him. He had not been able to look at Anne. When he did raise his face, he saw that she was watching him closely, like a mother who has just explained a disappointment to her child. Then he knew that he was no longer a part of Anne's world; responsible to the last, she had severed their connection in language which he could not fail to understand. He had failed her, and now he was being allotted his new status. It was like a confirmation, with boundaries and vows described; but he felt as though his new identity was like a prison.

Despite this, he had helped Anne with her luggage when she caught the London train, from the platform at Worthing station where they had first met. It was a Sunday afternoon in late July; the station was quiet, drowsing in the sun. Down the line, a heat-haze shimmered above the tracks.

'It's stupid you waiting,' Anne had said.

'I'd rather, really . . .'

'But what if I'd rather you didn't?'

'I . . .' John had not known what to say, but watched a young woman, weighed down with a heavy rucksack, as she wheeled her bicycle down the platform. He would leave, he had decided, when the woman stopped. Then, as anger overcame his sadness, he had left anyway, without saying goodbye. He had walked half a mile, the sunny, empty streets a blur, before running back to ask forgiveness, or at least see Anne once more. But by the time that he reached the station, hot and out of breath, the London train had gone. The platforms were empty once more, save for a man with a bucket and brush, who was whistling loudly as he slammed a door marked 'Private'. The emptiness was appalling.

Sarah, who knew the story of Anne's departure, and thought it sad but best accepted, wished that her cousin could let the matter drop.

'Just try to let it go,' she said, unlocking the door of her car, 'I'll call you later.' John nodded, and stepped back from the curb.

The Chatham stood in Hill Street, on the eastern edge of Mayfair. It was an undistinguished club, housed in an early Victorian terrace. An arch of black iron, with a box lantern at its centre, spanned the club steps; eight long windows looked down from the tall, narrow building to the street. The club had connections with law and medicine, but it had fallen on hard times. John's father had been a member, having once read law, and during his feeble last years he had had his son elected to the club for what he called a coming of age present. As an incompetent student of medicine, who had abandoned his training at a London hospital after only two years, John had used The Chatham quite regularly; he had taken his friends to dine there, he had learned the games of bridge and billiards from some of its older members. Once he had realised that his medical training was a failure, he had used the club as an excuse for idleness, an archaic retreat, and the inevitable destination of many purposeless walks. In those days, John's melancholy had matured both on the London streets and in the library and bar of The Chatham. The smell of leather, waxed panelling, cigar smoke and alcohol, blended with the odour, in winter, of scorched fabric as the club's heavy velvet curtains were draped to either side of scalding cast-iron radiators, was associated in John's mind with the twilight of his protracted youth. Within that heavy atmosphere, John and his friends had taken their pleasures seriously, self-consciously rehearsing what they assumed to be the manners of elder professional men. Initially, John had read the medical journals as he sipped his beer or whisky; later, when he had given up his courses, and he was used to being at a loose end, he was sure that the senior members must notice his obvious boredom, as he toyed with easy crosswords and read science fiction novels. John, whilst having a great capacity for pleasure, was lazy and easily bored. He had been brought up to this condition.

Making his way through Piccadilly, after his dinner with Sarah, John felt once more the aimless melancholy that had marked the last months of his previous residence in London. The difference, now, was morbid nervousness: each of his senses seemed incapable of filtering information to his mind without causing him anxiety. He had become physically self-conscious, to an acute degree, no longer able to respond unquestioningly to his surroundings and actions, but always aware that he was seeing, hearing, tasting, touching or inhaling. He imagined the physiological structure of his eyes – the core of his perception and his consciousness. He was forced to take each day in easy stages, but was terrified that he would find, soon, that the mere thought of having to live would overwhelm him. At first, his doctor had spoken of protohysteria, and agitated clinical depression. He had given John pills, Prozac, propranolol, diazepam, and instructed him as to the side-effects and qualities of each. 'This too will pass,' he had said, sympathetically, to his patient. John, meanwhile, held his days together with drugs. For seven years his life had been Anne; she had been his occupation; he had followed no other career. 'Depression is repressed rage,' a counsellor had told him; 'What are you so angry about?'. But John did not know. After his father had died, quiet with pain-killers, and hopeful that he would join his wife, incredibly drowned a decade earlier, John had sold The Beaumont Hotel which had been his inheritance. The hotel stood on Worthing's Marine Parade, not far from the pier. It had been in his father's family since 1912. His friends had told him that he had landed on his feet. He had seen no reason to move. He had just bought a house, and invested the remainder of his capital, when he met Anne. Deeply in love, they were going to travel.

Piccadilly Circus seemed larger at night. The automatic patterns of the high illuminated signs pursued their bright shapes, spelling out brand names in primary colours against their hoardings of darkness. The shops and restaurants were still busy; the rain had finally stopped. John crossed the road, as though he was superstitious of walking near the place where he had seen Anne. He wanted to know what film she had been going to see, but he turned his gaze instead towards the upper windows of Shaftesbury Avenue, above the pavement artists and the all-night pizza vendors. The windows were dark beneath black gables. Skirting the entrance of a large pharmacy, bathed in milk-white light, he reached the foot of Regent Street and passed by three fluorescent cards, each one the size of a door, which were hanging in the window of a record shop. The slabs of acid green and dayglo pink seemed to heighten the carnival atmosphere of the shops and crowds; the carnival, to John, was somehow soiled. He turned towards the quieter streets, where the shops were expensive and displayed their treasure of oil paintings and jewels behind railings and bullet-proof glass. The colour of the streets, too, began to change, from the grey and soft gold of Bond Street, on west to the pale blue of Mayfair, where there seemed to be no people at all.

Mayfair, to John, was the eye of London's storm; at night, the intricate maze of streets was perfectly still, all local bustle confined to the fairy-lit precincts of Shepherd

Market, to the south, which resembled a miniature Mediterranean town. But the heart of old Mayfair, of red-brick mansion flats and stucco-fronted terraces, disguising hundreds of discreet offices and private apartments, appeared far larger than its boundaries would allow. Amidst the evergreen shadows and the silence of wealth, it was a place where one could get lost, and find oneself in the shadow of a Park Lane hotel, or following a street that one had never seen before. Quiet and emptiness, at night, hung over the institutional streets of Mayfair, a sudden calm within the metropolitan roar. John was sure of his bearings, but he chose a deliberately obscure route. He wanted to delay the moment when he must return to his airless little bedroom, with its view of roof-tiles and pipes. Alone in South Audley Street, he listened to the sound of his own footsteps.

Anne had always liked London, and defended its merits as only a Londoner could. Born and raised in Battersea, an only child, she had made a thorough exploration of the capital by the time she reached her eighteenth birthday. At weekends she would set off to distant areas of the city and see whatever there was to be seen: a Victorian pumping station, a canal, a cemetery, a park, a museum – her destinations were varied. On leaving college, where she had studied Hotel Management, she took a further qualification in the French language and then worked for nine months in Switzerland. This done, she acquainted herself with Europe in much the same manner as she had London. At twenty-one years old, when John was wasting his time and his father's money in The Chatham,

Anne was fully independent, and her clear eyes were fixed on more distant, more exotic horizons. She toured America and then the Far East, working her way to Australia, where she wintered beside a white beach. She became intimate with the world: watching sunsets, touring cities, admiring waterfalls, glimpsing deserts and jungles. From country to country and from city to city, she collected experience as other young people might collect qualifications, or save the money to buy a car. When she finally returned to England, shortly before her twenty-third birthday, she found London small and her parents' home oppressive. She took a job in Victoria Street, on a good salary, assisting with the organisation of an International Conference fund, and then her life was changed by John.

The wet May morning on Worthing station was vivid in John's mind, brought back to him by the scent of rain and damp streets, as he let himself into the dark hall of The Chatham with his night-key. It was just midnight. Through the tall panelled doors to his right, John could hear the clinking of glasses and the low male grumble of conversation and laughter. The smell of cigar smoke was acrid, drifting in blue ribbons through the dim wedge of light which fell across the black and white marble of the floor. John saw the shadowy outline of himself in the gilded and tarnished mirror which hung above the foot of the broad staircase. The doors to the library were shut; the porter's vacant desk was illuminated as though by candlelight. John couldn't face the bar, and made his way to his room, running his palm along the wide waxed rail of the heavy banister. The elderly carpet muffled his steps, and he ascended into silence.

The argument, within minutes, had established an intimate dialogue between John White and Anne Champney; the fatuous disagreement over Anne's lost umbrella had become the first friend, and genius, of their love. Like strangers meeting in a distant foreign country, who discover that they speak the same language while all around is an alien, obscure culture, the couple had felt relief and generosity at each new statement and inflection. The guttering on the station canopy had burst, suddenly showering the platform with rain-water, and Anne had rushed into John's arms to avoid being soaked. 'What a dynamic entrance,' she had quipped. Some months later, as she lay in his embrace, she told him that his charm had been like an electrical current. 'But with your eyes,' she had added, 'you could do anything – have anyone . . .'

'But I want you . . .'

'And you've got me . . .'

Anne had never fallen in love before. She had felt sympathetic towards certain men, or attracted, fleetingly, to brief seductions, but she had never felt her world changed, as though physically, by love. She found John beautiful; she was almost ashamed of the simplicity of her response to him. She would trace his lips with her finger, and say 'Oh dear . . .', before resting her head against his chest and closing her eyes. Love, to Anne, was rare and absolute; to love and be loved in return was a gift which granted security and strength – it opened the world and enabled the best of life to be shared. Love could enrich as well as protect; it was a crime to waste one minute in thoughts and actions which were not worthy of love. But Anne would never speak this philosophy; she was a realist and a pragmatist who preferred actions to analysis. John, however, was lazy, and he had taken too much for granted. Pleasure, as he had known it, was a sun-drenched plateau which stretched to hazy horizons; it demanded no effort, and promised few surprises. It was a form of comfortable enervation.

The club bedrooms were small and sparsely furnished. There were ten in all, seven of which opened off a dark corridor on the third floor, and three more in the attic, in disused servants' quarters. John had taken a room in the attic. The upper floors of The Chatham were quiet, save for the distant roar and hiss of the antiquated plumbing, and the occasional groan of a loose floorboard on the lower landing. Very little daylight reached the corridors; there were weak, unshaded bulbs, dangling from the high ceiling on cord flexes, which were turned on and off by ancient bakelite time-switches. A strip of carpet, which had once been green but was now worn away to matting, led to the foot of the attic stairs. There was a rich odour of wax polish, made musty and airless by dust. The walls had not been painted for years; there were no paintings or prints. But the bedroom doors were made of panelled mahogany, and their brass handles and finger-plates gleamed dully in the crepuscular gloom. On summer afternoons, when the sunshine fell through a small skylight, set high above the stairwell, these upper corridors seemed even more remote and forlorn than they did during the brief twilights of mid-winter.

John made his way up the steep attic stairs, which twisted sharply, and gained his room in darkness. The old lock turned noisily and the door swung open to a cramped, plain room, the low ceiling of which was sloped in accordance with the erratic contours of the roof. A sash window, broader than it was high, gave a view of slates and chimneys; half a mile away, the lights in the symmetrical rooms of a modern hotel looked warm and inviting, suggesting the security of busy travellers whose lives were serviced by efficient comforts.

Used to the darkness, John sat down on the sagging bed. He did not turn on the light. The bed was narrow; ladies, even wives, were not allowed to stay on the club's premises. Once, John had smuggled Anne to his room and she had been erotically complicit with this infringement of The Chatham's rules. She had behaved like an urbane mistress – the only woman in a male enclave, laughing at authority to be with her lover. Initially shy, and modest by nature, Anne's passion had grown stronger with time; during the early years of marriage, she had swiftly taken the lead in their love-making. Each scene and each caress, each mannerism and each endearment, now, would return to John with unbearable clarity; he was forced to close his eyes, tightly, as though to dispel their magic.

Sighing, John pulled his old leather holdall out from under the bed, and rummaged with one hand amongst its contents. He threw a clean shirt towards the faded basket chair which stood beside the window, its back caught by a stray shaft of orange light. Then, finding his sponge-bag, he took out a bottle of pills, setting them carefully on the low wooden dresser. A bottle of tepid mineral water, which he had opened the previous night, stood to one side. Finally, he took out a small towel, and released from its folds a china figurine of a forces sweetheart, clad in her underwear and standing with her hands placed coquettishly on her hips. The piece was an antique; John had found it in a box filled with old ledgers, rubber-stamps and discoloured envelopes, in the basement of his father's hotel. There was something in the posture of the statuette, and a freak coincidence in its manufactured expression, which reminded him of Anne. No specific detail of the figure was faithful to his wife's features; it was the bearing of the whole, when glimpsed, which caused a sad rush of affection. John placed the figurine on the other side of the pills, and lit a cigarette.

At night, John found, he could roam more easily through his thoughts. He crossed the small room, stooping slightly, and pushed open the stiff sash window by jerking the lower frame upwards with his palms. The paintwork cracked, and the window rattled loudly as it opened. Moist, leaf-scented air blew into the room; a fragrant breeze cut through the smell of stale smoke. Picking up his pills and water, John sat down in the chair by the window. He leaned back, resting his head on the sill, and breathed the night air with pleasure. He had come to enjoy the last hour of his day, because the two diazepam tablets which he took — usually with a cup of sweet tea – had the initial effect of slowing his thoughts and loosening his muscles, and of making the half-light intimate. The two small white pills, chalky and seemingly weightless, were like bland friends. John swallowed them down with the warm water, and then rinsed his mouth with a second sip. The pills would dry his mouth, later, so he saved the remains of the water. He knew that it would take fifteen minutes before his mind would relax and his limbs would grow heavy, and he would feel content to be falling into grey, dreamless sleep. The unbearable pain of knowing that Anne, incredibly, no longer loved him, and that being awake was a battle, would become abstract. He lit a fresh cigarette and smoked it slowly, gazing at a patch of bronze light above the bed. He knew that when he stood up, his legs would be weak and he would stumble to bed.

In Worthing, John and Anne had shared a vast bed which was set well away from the wall. Their tall house, with its pillared entrance and blue tiled balcony, stood at the end of a promenade terrace, just half a mile from where the sealed and abandoned hulk of John's father's hotel had awaited demolition. It was quiet, comfortable and slightly shabby. The youthful clamour of Brighton reached Worthing as a genteel echo, filtered through the busier streets of Hove. The promenade at Worthing, from October to March, was like a broad stretch of silence, the modest pier shuttered and the sea like an indifferent guest. The vestiges of seaside carnival, expressed in ornate wind-shelters, quiet cafés, the glass-fronted amusement arcade and the white sea-facing facades of small hotels and boarding houses, served only to ease the resort deeper into its doze. This doze was disturbed, in part, by the trappings of a modern town centre and restored grandeur; the two atmospheres lay side by side, almost denying each other . . . At night, along the coastal road, the lights which glimmered on the hotels and bars appeared like minute circles of pink and scarlet, floating in blue darkness. In June, when the placid, milky sea was revealed at first light, the lines of sunshine would spread across the low waves, seeming to jump and flash as the promenade, deserted and still, awaited activity. The sea air would be fresh and strong, and then the heat would begin. The sunshine, glinting on glass and iron, would find out obscure corners . . .

John's eyelids were growing heavy, and his breathing was soft and regular. The succession of anxieties which had formed his day – the incision of the wet streets and buildings into his speculations, and then the sudden glimpse of Anne – were beginning to melt. Had he really seen her? He was almost sure that he had. He thought of his empty house: the cover on the bed smoothed flat, the stairs quiet, the flowers in the drawing-room wilted and russet. He reproached himself, once more, for failing to recognise how devoted Anne had been to nurturing their love. His thoughts grew confused, but pleasantly; he tried to remember how Anne had phrased her goodbyes: 'I tried so hard, John; I loved you so very much, but I've grown so tired of trying . . .' How could he have failed to notice that he was giving his wife nothing in return for her love? They had travelled, they had settled . . .

The phone rang sharply beside John's bed. Its bell made a harsh, shrill rasping which cut through the quiet. John half-tumbled across the small room and grabbed at the receiver. His mind was trying to catch up with the sudden disturbance.

'Hello?'

'John? It's Sarah; I was just ringing to check that you're okay.'

John cleared his throat, and coughed. 'I'm sorry; hi. I was half asleep.'

'I'll let you get back to bed.' said Sarah. 'I was just ringing, to check . . .'

'It's kind of you . . .'

'What are you doing tomorrow?'

John's mind was blank. He couldn't remember what day it was. 'I'm, oh, I'm going to the Flower Show with Tony.'

There was a pause. 'The Flower Show?' said Sarah, surprised; 'Which flower show?'

'I thought it was the Flower Show,' said John, panicking slightly as he tried to gather his thoughts. 'I must have got the day wrong.'

'I think you've got the month wrong.' Sarah sighed. 'Listen, Robert says we must have you over for dinner before you leave. Are you free on Sunday evening?'

'I'm not sure . . .'

'Tomorrow's Saturday.'

John relaxed; 'Yes; I'm free on Sunday . . . Sorry.'

'At around eight then; you've got the address?'

'Unless you've moved – '

'No; we're here. John?'

'Yes?'

'Try to be okay when everything isn't okay; that's what we've all got to do . . .'

'I know. Thanks . . . Give my love to Robert.'

'We'll see you on Sunday. And call – if you need anything. All right?'

'Thanks Sarah; good night . . .'

John replaced the receiver and lay down on his bed. He would undress, soon, and make a list in his mind of all the places where he'd been happy. He fell asleep thinking of Madrid, where Anne had bought a black belt. The window rattled gently in the breeze, and a taxi shuddered to a halt in the mews. London continued while John slept.

Two

Towards the end of the 1980s, Sarah Vick had jumped ship from a sinking merchant bank. She had then managed to clamber on board a rival financial institution whose fortunes were rapidly rising. With regard to her daily routine, this meant that Sarah now faced, through the windows of her new office, on the north-western corner of Blackfriars Bridge, the partially hidden penthouse suites of her old office, which stood on the southern bank of the river, and now seemed far away. Since the crash of '87, Sarah had noticed a severe change in the attitudes of the City: many of the old hierarchies and prejudices had returned; senior staff could be counted upon to have similar accents and similar qualifications; many of the new firms had swiftly collapsed, leaving in their wake entire floors of abandoned office space and drifts of unopened mail. What was left, or what had returned, was a harder, less flamboyant type of City employee. It was rather as though, after a colourful but ultimately disastrous campaign, a mercenary army had been discharged with no pay, and the professional soldiers had marched on – serving their old generals, submitting to old rules, and trying to forget that they had ever allowed themselves the indulgence of a brief springtime of anarchy. Sarah, dressed in a sober grey suit, was glad to be at least an officer within the command of the new regime.

Sarah's boyfriend, Robert Marshall, was an idealist. An architect by profession, but a politician by nature, he was committed to the division, within new building schemes, of space for community and public use as well as private development. He spent much of his time in meetings. Sometimes, when the round of meetings drew to an end, he would discover that he had been successful, and that a floor of workshop units – marked down for low rental – would be incorporated within the premises of a prestigious company headquarters. On other occasions, the meetings would not proceed so well, and Robert would report his failure back to Sarah in short, bitter sentences. Robert was forty years old, and Sarah was one year younger; they had bought a flat in the Barbican Centre shortly after they had first met, ten years earlier.

The circumstances of their meeting, and of their subsequent purchase of the high, slightly cramped apartment, had been so level as to pass almost unnoticed by their friends. It had been winter; Robert and Sarah, in the first flush of attraction, had attended a concert of music by Stockhausen in the Barbican Centre hall. During the first half of the concert they had listened carefully; in the interval, over glasses of red wine, they had found that they shared an equally serious outlook on life: art and travel were to be appreciated, business ought to recognise its social responsibilities, governments, in general, were not to be trusted. They had returned to their seats as more than comrades; they had awakened passion in one another, and a far-reaching mutual trust. When they left the hall, wrapped against the cold in scarves and long coats, they had paused to look at the ice which had formed on the water-gardens. Robert had gingerly tested the frozen surface with his toe; Sarah, breathless, had held him by the sleeve.

'One false move and you'd go through,' Robert had announced, without humour.

Looking up at the residential towers, with their lipped balconies like opened drawers, Sarah had said how marvellous it would be to live in one of the high apartments.

'And the views must be spectacular,' Robert had said, adding, 'This whole place is a classic of its kind.'

Sarah had nodded, and smiled at Robert; his eyes were glinting enthusiastically behind the lenses of his glasses. By the following summer, the couple were settled in a twelfth floor apartment which commanded a view of St Paul's cathedral and Bankside Power Station. They were proud of their purchase, and of their view, in particular. Solid, hard-working, liberal and prosperous, they set about the business of living. They had no desire to get married, and Sarah could not have any children. They discussed the possibility of adopting a child; but while their desire to be good foster parents was sincere, the adoption agencies were not convinced that the couple would be suited to carrying out their intentions. After this rebuff, their professional careers had leapt forward.

Sarah's relations with her cousin, John, had taken time to achieve a sharpness of focus. John was ten years her junior, and meeting him as a student – away from the rituals of family anniversaries and parties – she had found him dull. It was only after he had met Anne, and brought her to visit his cousin and her partner, that Sarah had detected in John the makings of a new companion, with thoughts and aspirations which she could, as she said, respect. Anne had seemed mature and interesting. Sarah had been expecting, half-heartedly, a bubbly young girl and she found herself surprised and impressed by the tall, dark-haired woman who accepted a glass of Irish whisky with the assurance of a well-travelled adult.

During that first meeting, Sarah had studied John's face as he followed every word and inflection of his girl-friend's well-turned anecdotes. John had never been a person upon whom Sarah would rely at dinner parties; his conversation, in the past, had tended to be limited and slow, as though purely reactive, and lacking in wit or opinion. To Sarah's way of thinking, a person ought either to possess wit or opinions; her own friends, she believed, could claim both. But John, she felt, had been spoiled, by his father's indulgence and a lack of ambition.

The younger family, John, Sarah, her sister, Joanne – had grown up with the old age and failings of David White's Beaumont Hotel. The Beaumont's long, dark corridors, smelling of cigarette smoke, talcum powder and cooking, had been John's labyrinthine childhood home, and his kingdom to share with playmates. Even during the late 1960s, the hotel had catered for fewer and fewer families; there was an increasing number of elderly and infirm residents, who slumbered throughout the long afternoons in the warm glass-fronted lounge, and climbed the stairs at a feeble pace, passing into darkness like tired ghosts. John had run and played, being fed sweets by sentimental old ladies. Even after his father's death, and the sale of the Beaumont to speculators in property, it had required Anne Champney to turn the pretty boy into a handsome man, with some will of his own. Sarah had sometimes wondered whether being raised in an hotel was at the root of both John's charm and his neurosis. Whatever the case, no man, it seemed, could do better for himself than marry such a woman as Anne.

It had been said, but not with malice, that Anne was handsome as opposed to pretty. To John, of course, she was far more than that: pale and fine-featured, with brown eyes, a small, delicate mouth, and a figure which was slender to the point of fragility, Anne lacked the smooth prettiness which is ascribed to feminine beauty; instead, she possessed an angular strength of profile, and a subtle grace, which, when revealed, would animate her presence like the sun coming out over a soft but austere landscape. She was aware of this double mechanism within her appearance; her ability, at will, to become mesmeric and arresting — but she minded this power with care, which increased its potency. Secure in her wit and her experience, but more eloquent to an audience than to individuals, she was a woman whose personality exposed her to attention. She could flirt, successfully, resting her chin on the fingers of her left hand (her nails exquisitely manicured and painted) as she spoke in a voice that was amused and seductively low. In arguments, she would allow her opponent to declare himself fully, and passionately, before harrying his thesis with a few facts, or a contrary point of view, which would shift the debate into new and unexpected territory. After such bouts she would usually leave admired. But beneath Anne's confidence and her clarity of thought and ambition, there was a core of sensitivity which could make her swift to take offence, or incline her towards deep pessimism. She had suffered, at times, for her reputation for suave sagacity. She would reason her position in silence, more often than not, but having reached a decision was fearless in making her view known. Above all, she was incapable of telling a lie.

When Sarah reached home, after her dinner with John, she felt as though her neat day had been spoiled, like a present dropped. The high apartment was dark and warm. She unbuttoned her jacket and dropped her bag on a chair. The long lounge window, uncurtained, was an oblong of blue, floating at the end of the unlit room. Robert was still out, working late. Turning on the low lamp which stood on a glass-topped table, Sarah heard the urgent electronic purr of the telephone. It was Robert, calling from his office, affectionate but weary.

'How was your evening?' he asked, stifling a yawn.

'I saw John – '

'Our John?'

'He called the office just as I was leaving. He'd seen Anne . . .'

'Really?' Robert's tone lifted. 'I didn't even know he was in town; and he met Anne?'

'He saw Anne – going into a cinema, with some man . . .'

'Oh.' Robert sounded disappointed. He sighed. 'Well, it's her life . . .'

'Exactly. But John's in such an awful state. It's horrible. I couldn't think of what to say. I mean, what can you say? Loads of people get divorced, or split up, and it's never nice . . .'

'Guy and Clara were quite happy about it . . .'

'That was different.'

'But they had such a weird relationship anyway. Is Clara still seeing her therapist?'

'I don't know . . .' Sarah stretched. 'Have you eaten?'

'I had some sandwiches, around six . . .'

'You must be starving. When will you be back?'

'Soon. Now. I'm just leaving . . .'

'We can sleep in tomorrow . . .'

There was a pause. Sarah slipped off her shoes and curled up in a corner of the deep sofa, cradling the telephone receiver beneath her chin.

'I'd like to see John.' said Robert, emphatically, 'Why don't we ask him over for dinner, on Sunday?'

'With Roger and April?'

'Why not? I think they'd get on. Ask him . . .'

'Okay; I'll try and catch him now . . .'

Robert and Sarah exchanged kisses down the telephone. Sarah poured herself a glass of wine and then stood beside the window, looking at the buildings and the lights. She was glad that Robert was so dependable; he drew his strength from his work, as she did, and together they seemed to weather the storms of growing old by relying upon one another, joint navigators of their small but comfortable craft. Their private world, though not perfect, was intact; they could treat themselves, over the years, to a ripening and calming of their original desires; they had their high flat, and a slightly bigger car than they needed; they would buy, eventually, a second home in Spain or Italy, which they would work upon and retire to, one day, to read and garden and entertain their friends. Their lives would never be dramatic, or marked by grand gestures, but they would be comfortable. More and more, Sarah felt, the business of living was to find modest comfort with a person whom one loved. The bigger prizes, the ones that people became ill, or corrupt, to win, had not lost their lustre but had lost their desirability. 'I'm good at my job,' she thought, watching the white lights of a car and the red lights of a lorry, 'but I wouldn't want to run the whole company.'

The night sky, as seen from Sarah's window, was broken into three layers of light: at the highest point, opaque darkness was marked by the tiny scarlet dots of an airliner; beneath this, the reflected lights of London made an artificial ceiling of pale violet gauze, mottled by the undersides of drifting clouds; then there was the lower band of blue, streaked with sodium orange, and this broke up at street-level into blocks of shadow and clusters of neon. The dome of St Paul's was bathed in peach-coloured light, its walls and pillars still floodlit. Sarah thought of all the activity that her view represented, and could see a method and a harmony within it. John, she believed, could find no rest because he had no method; Anne had carried him, and now he was floundering.

She returned to the telephone and called her cousin. She was pleased that he would be free for dinner; it made her feel that she had done something.

John woke early and suddenly. There was no middle drowsiness as he surfaced from sleep; consciousness returned like a light being switched on, without the luxury of tiredness or sleepily wandering thoughts. Awakening was absolute: a thrust into anxiety. As his eyes snapped open, he began to tremble; his muscles convulsed and he rubbed his legs together and clenched his toes, as if to work off the nervousness which was disturbing his body. He was lying on his stomach with the coarse sheet wrapped tightly over his shoulder and a heavy blanket weighing on his hips. The daylight, insisting that another day could not be hurried on to night and a further chance to sleep, appeared despotic and cruel – a photographic whiteness which prompted the nausea of fear. John could feel two hot furrows of pain, burning the nape of his neck and driving a deep line to the small of his back. Still shaking he closed his eyes, imagining a madness of hypermania. He told himself that every day began with this pain and fear, but that night would eventually come and with it the dread might lessen. But the fear was immediate, and John could no longer lie still; he looked at his watch – it was a few minutes before five o'clock in the morning. His eyes felt tight within their sockets and all thought was threatening; his senses felt too alert, as though his nervous system would short-circuit with the mere strain of being awake. For the previous five months, since he had known that Anne was settled in London, John had responded to his circumstances with a self-fuelling cycle of anxiety and depression. The thought that his Anne no longer wanted to have anything to do with him, and that the greatest privilege, of trust, had been withdrawn, increased his self-pity and his weakness. He had come to think of his life in terms of his problem. Sarah thought this was a common complaint.

He pulled on his clothes and shoes – a clean white shirt, fresh from its packet, his black suit, a pair of weathered brogues – and collected his cigarettes, money and pills from the dresser. He moved slowly, with a stoop, unable to straighten his back and face the day directly. The anxiety had induced a state of acute self-consciousness, with distortions of perspective which created – or seemed to – a gap between John's senses and his surroundings. His responses were a heartbeat too early or too late; he felt as though he was distanced from reality by a sheet of thick glass. His doctor had told him, kindly, that such sensations could be the side-effects of anti-depressants and mood-brighteners. 'If that is the cure,' Robert had said, 'how dreadful must be the affliction.' But, for John, it was hard to distinguish between his condition and the chemicals which helped him to bear it. Every move and decision required effort; his mouth was dry and his heart was pounding. He would walk to the coffee shop of the nearest big hotel and try to steady his nerves. His days required strict but gentle organisation; his confidence, each morning, had to be slowly renewed.

The club was silent as John descended the broad, half-lit stairs. The porter would not come on duty for another two hours. Staff and members were still asleep; there were probably no more than six people in the building. The stillness of the club was intense: it weighed upon the unwashed glasses and blackened cigar ends left over from the previous night; it hung in the grey gloom of the hall, and the unexpected brightness of the tall-windowed dining room. As John pulled open the heavy door, catching his thumb in the brass lock, he was surprised by the fresh air on his face and the high, uneven whistle of birdsong. Hill Street was quiet, but the distant urgency of a few cars, speeding down the emptiness of Park Lane, could be heard as a low roar.

The day was not sunny, but the morning light was luminous and bright. John put on his dark glasses, and was comforted by the constriction of his vision within their moss-green lenses. There was a slight chill in the air; the streets and buildings were damp. He walked through the deserted roads towards South Audley Street. Display lights and adverts were still gleaming weakly in some of the shop windows. A fan of pale pink blossom had drifted across the pavement, the edges of the petals mingled with dust. As he reached Grosvenor Square, and exchanged the silence of Mayfair for the busier precincts of Oxford Street, where buses were already rumbling and the shops appeared to be dozing, in preparation for the business of Saturday, John felt once more like a burglar breaking into Anne's house. He pictured her asleep, her knees drawn up towards her stomach, and her eyelashes dark against her cheeks. She would be warm to hold, her lips set in a serious expression. John looked at the empty square; the tall trees were coming into leaf, obscuring the dull red brick of the offices which enclosed its northern side; the fountains seemed lonely and forlorn. The gates to the square were still locked; the empty lawns looked fresh and trim. Thick-headed and weary, John walked on towards The Marriott Hotel, where the brasserie never closed. He wished that he could enjoy himself; he had lost the ability to look forward to anything; that capacity withdrawn, emptiness echoed emptiness, and he felt that he was nothing more than a useless body, driven by the ghost of a personality.

The lobby of The Marriott, carpeted in pale blue and divided by pillars of saffron-shaded marble, was warm and quiet. The air-conditioned atmosphere was rich with the scents of an expensive hotel; slivers of sweetness, as though from a newly opened bottle of perfume, laced the warm odour of cleaned upholstery, this mixture being tinged with a refined trace of alcohol. Rosewood cabinets, containing illuminated stands of beige velvet, displayed crystal foals and gold watches; the concierge, standing with his hands behind his back, nodded to John as he passed by. The night receptionist, her long brown hair tied up in a bow of blue ribbon, was studying the screen of a computer; her pale face, set in an expression of deep concentration, was bathed in green light as she tapped her pen against her teeth. John, running his fingers through his tangled hair, nodded briefly as he strode towards the shallow flight of stairs which lead to the brasserie. Two Arabs, dressed in white shirts and brown linen trousers, were murmuring together in the dark corridor which marked the discreet entrance to the cloakrooms. This corridor, windowless and decorated with large, ebony-framed prints, depicting botanical specimens, was silent; the carpeted floors and walls absorbed all sound. John, preparing to wash before he ordered his tea and orange juice, pushed open the heavy door of the cloakroom with his shoulder.

The white wash-basins were set in a slab of grey marble; two were already filled with hot water, a folded hand-towel lying ready to one side. Bottles of still water, their blue caps loosened, gleamed before the dark mirrors. John bought a disposable toothbrush, its nylon bristles impregnated with mint paste, from a low dispenser which was fastened on the far wall. Taking off his jacket, he splashed his face with warm water; he would bathe at The Chatham, in more elderly surroundings, later on. The warm water eased the soreness around his eyes but did not revive him; he washed once more with cold water, and then brushed his teeth, vigorously scrubbing and spitting. This activity caused him to retch – a painful buckling in his throat and chest. He thought that he was going to faint. He steadied himself against the marble slab, feeling its coolness on his hot palms. His eyes were watering. Breathing more slowly, he looked up and studied his face in the mirror. It was an undeniably handsome face, but flawed: lean and lightly tanned, his skin was

44

beginning to show creases of worry across his forehead; violet-coloured semi-circles drooped beneath his blue eyes. Two days' growth of beard darkened his chin and jaw. He thought that he looked seedy. His blond hair, the colour of drying thatch, needed cutting. He took out his comb and pulled his fringe into a parting. He looked more presentable, but knots of tension in his back and shoulders gave him a hunched and weary attitude. He straightened his back and looked himself in the eyes as he stared at his reflection. He felt entombed within his own body; the cloakroom seemed like a blue nighttime behind him.

Turning to leave, John picked up a small flask of courtesy cologne; splashing the clear liquid on his palms, and slapping his face with the scent, his senses recoiled to the precise perfume of a particular memory: the cologne, untitled, was heavily aromatic, its strongest ingredient conveyed the peppery, incense laden atmosphere of the interior of an Italian church. The fragrance was exact: a scent like hot stone, flowers, candles and antiquity. It was rich with ecclesiastical subtlety and the suggestion of ritual and mysticism. To John, the cologne recreated the happiness of a romance; in the mingling of musk, cinnamon, frankincense and rosewood, he was taken back to a morning of glaring white sunlight, and the airless cool of a church in a small town not far from Naples. Anne had known all about the church; she had pointed out the medieval carvings of birds and elephants which she had seen once before on her own earlier travels. She had been wearing white trousers and a blue shirt; her lipstick had been pale. Her smooth, slender hand had reached out to his, absentmindedly, through the pungent half-light.

John stared uselessly at the tiles of the cloakroom floor; he wished that he could rub off the cologne, but it had already soaked into his collar. The memories, vivid in the clinging scent, inspired one another: a bend on a dusty road, scorched grass giving way to the white-gold glister of a bay; an indifferent meal, eaten in splendid isolation on a grand, deserted balcony, in the deep blue of late evening; a hot, plain bedroom, with two chairs pulled up to the tall window, which faced the slow sunset . . . John dried his hands and turned away from the mirror. A phrase had come into his mind, splintered from the hard words of a more recent conversation with Anne. Why had he tried to contact her, as though he was already capable of being her friend? But his acting had been too successful; laughing, Anne had told him: 'Someone at work called me a flirt the other day!' For John this was unbearable; a dance upon the grave of his hopes. His stomach cold, he left the silent cloakroom.

The Marriott brasserie, with its twenty-four-hour menu displayed on a gold lectern beside the smoked glass doors of its entrance, was bright with sudden sunshine. John was shown to a table by the window, which looked out over the lawns of Grosvenor Square. The brasserie was low-ceilinged, but ornate – a blur of pink and gold; the table linen, napkins and lampshades were all a shade of dusty peach; a triple-tiered trolley, incongruous in the slow atmosphere of early morning, displayed trays of cream-topped gateaux and shallow bowls of fruit salad.

It was like dining at an airport, between time-zones. In the furthest corner of the room, a quiet family of Americans were eating cooked breakfasts, the heavy jowled father leaning forward to engage with his laden fork. John couldn't see any other diners. An oriental waiter took his order for tea, orange juice and a sweet pastry. He leaned back in his chair, feeling ill at ease. The light was falling across his face; he studied the fussy arrangement of cutlery, condiments, flower-vase and crockery which crowded his table. The single pink carnation appeared pale beside its strand of nylon fern; the crystal ashtray was spotless, reflecting a rainbow-coloured prism across the breadth of its shadow.

A young woman, fresh from her shower but still tired, came into the brasserie; her oval face was expressionless, her wet blonde hair was combed back, flat and scented over her head. She was wearing three heavy rings, one on top of the other, and a collarless dress like a shift. She looked continental, but she ordered her breakfast in a low, Northern accent. Absorbed in her thoughts, she stared at the table cloth whilst stroking her lips with a stick of white salve. She glanced at John, but did not register his presence. John, of late, had been troubled by the irrational thought that one cannot see oneself being seen; eyes, however eloquent or filled with life, could sometimes seem to him, morbidly, as blank solids. His friend Tony, with whom he had once studied medicine, and who was now a clinical psychologist, had made some observations about this fear of eyes. Today, John remembered, was Tony's day: they were due to meet at The

47

Chatham at noon. Looking at the young woman once more, he saw two light blemishes which marked her back to the right of her spine; her loose, backless dress displayed the delicate shadows of her vertebrae, shifting as she reached down to her bag. The waiter arrived with John's breakfast, a meaningless smile playing around his lips. He set down the juice and the tea quite firmly, twisting each jug and glass as it touched the table cloth. The pastry, wrapped in a pink napkin, was placed on the furthest edge of the table.

'Enjoy your breakfast, sir,' he said. 'Can I get you a paper?'

John shook his head and poured some tea.

With Anne, in Worthing, they had breakfasted at weekends on warm brioche, bought from the supermarket the night before; lavender honey was folded onto the saltless, white butter, this sweet mixture melting on the cake-like bread. They had drunk strong coffee, which John had now been forced to give up. On some mornings, still drowsy, they had held one another whilst waiting for the kettle to boil. Now, instead of that ordinary happiness which had been so vast that he had taken it for granted, John had only the mediocre pastime of regret, and a nervous condition which bound his day to a neurotic routine. He called this routine his rut, and he was learning to love it. He drank down his orange juice in two long draughts, and then lit a cigarette. Reaching in his pocket, he took out a small bottle of propranolol tablets, which would lower his heart rate and calm him. He took one tablet with his second sip of sweet tea, and felt his system slow down. The blue smoke of his cigarette, curling in a thickening plume, hung in the pale gold spring sunshine which was falling across the table. John felt as though he had been up and working for hours. With tired eyes, he watched the inscrutable waiter, serving pink grapefruit to the solitary young woman from Manchester. The morning, like every morning, told John he was sick.

Tony Wollen was short and dapper. His thinning fair hair was combed back from his high forehead, and he wore clear-framed prescription glasses which gave a studious intensity to his boyish face. He spoke quickly, with a refined accent which seemed to curl the clauses of his sentences into tapering ironic statements. He enjoyed his job, referring to himself as a Harley Street shrink; his attitudes approached self-parody. He would sit low down in his chair, his legs loosely crossed, and tap his thumbs together as he held forth, or listened with seemingly rapt attention, scarcely blinking. As a student of John's year, he had been attracted to the good life; with John, he had gone to parties and indulged in drinking sprees; they had also played tennis together, in Hackney, and hired a boat to take them down to Greenwich on a floating picnic. But while John would simply roam from pleasure to pleasure, unconcerned by work or ambition, Tony had divided his time between hard study and what he considered to be the appropriate reward for that study. After John left, not missed by his tutors, Tony had begun to work in earnest. His speciality was the mind.

Now, at thirty-two years old, Tony was thought to

be a more than able clinical psychologist. He had trained in a large south London hospital, writing up his cases and contributing to the debate within his science. He possessed the intuition and the character to diagnose with speed and accuracy, quickly finding some relief for his patients. He believed in the talking cure, with some reliance upon drugs during the initial stages of treatment. Beneath his precocity and his brisk attitude he had a genuine sympathy for those with sick and troubled minds.

With regard to John, Tony was well aware that his friend's condition was not acute. At first, when John had become subordinate to the symptoms of a free-floating anxiety, and had lost his way in the labyrinth of stress-management and depression, Tony had steered him towards a consultant psychiatrist. But he was disinclined to speak with his friend professionally: 'You're seeing one doctor already,' he would say, 'and now you must follow her advice.' His purpose for meeting, that Saturday lunchtime, was to relax and enjoy himself. He was struck, however, by John's physical deterioration.

John had approached the meeting with misgiving; he felt ill, tired, and morbidly aware of his vision: he had the sense that his head was a hand-held camera, jerking from point to point; he felt disconnected. He fought back against his fear by repeating to himself: 'You have been all right; you have done nothing irrational; you are neur-otic, you are not psychotic . . .' Absorbed in these prob-lems he found concentration difficult, and then repro-ached himself for being poor company. He found Tony waiting for him in The Chatham bar. His friend was dressed in grey flannel trousers, a soft blue shirt and crimson tie, and a tweed jacket. He smiled when he saw John, and gestured in mock despair at the empty room.

'This place is always dead at the weekends,' said John, 'But I'll try and find you a drink.'

'A dry sherry, please.'

John strolled over to the vast mahogany bar which rose up like a high altar, its deep shelves crowded with dusty bottles and its mirrored back reflecting a long row of spirits. The surface of the bar was black and greasy with years of use. A young steward, dressed in a stained white jacket, emerged from the pantry drying his hands on a towel.

'Leaky keg, sir: what can I get you?'

John ordered a glass of dry sherry and a tumbler of fruit juice.

'You do know, sir,' said the steward, busying himself with glasses and bottles, 'that there's no club dinner tonight or tomorrow? Members are asked to dine out.'

'I know, thanks.'

'No staff at weekends, you see; there's not enough call . . .'

'That's fine.'

John picked up his drinks, and the steward returned to his leaking keg. At The Beaumont, he remembered, he had used to accompany the wine waiter on his missions to the half empty cellar. This had seemed an adventure: the racks stretched off into the gloom, the cool air was rich with an odour that the boy thought of as purple;

coal-black webs and dust stretched along the walls. Fifteen years later, when Anne and himself were inseparable, they had returned to the cellar and discovered two bottles of champagne. The hotel had been empty; the furniture and fittings had been sold off, the unlit rooms were dim and forlorn. But the damp walls, with their plaster motifs and dado rail, had absorbed sixty years of disparate lives, commingled and concentrated by the quiet routine of an English bourgeois hotel. A few chairs, covered by a dirty sheet, had been stacked in the dining-room. A faint smell of cooking still lingered. The couple's footsteps had echoed on the wooden floor.

'This was it,' John had said, stretching out his arms to the empty room.

'It must have been strange.'

'Not really; it was all I knew. What seemed really funny to other children was the fact that we never went on holiday ourselves; we didn't even go out much. Life was the hotel seasons, which was kind of insular, I suppose.'

Anne had found an old menu. 'Lunch,' she read out, 'soup of the day, fruit juice . . .'

'Prawn cocktail, pâté de maison . . .' continued John.

'So what seemed like a treat?'

'Going to school, then meeting girls, then . . . I don't know; my father was becoming more and more ill – nothing was normal. I couldn't get on.'

'Well, now you can look after me.'

'I wouldn't have thought that you need much looking after . . .'

'I adore you; oh, so much, I adore – you . . .'

John handed Tony his sherry and sat down on a straight-backed chair.

'Well, cheers.' Tony raised his glass and took a sip of sherry. John, nodding, inclined his tumbler towards Tony.

'It's incredible,' said Tony, 'that places like this still exist; when I come in here I feel as though there's something desperate and sad in the air. No offence.' he added, laughing.

'It's a bit like a nursing home;' said John, 'but the inmates don't know what they're suffering from. Booze and cigars in most cases. Except for all the noisy young men, who don't believe in illness.'

'Are you here for long?' asked Tony, glancing at the sunshine streaming through the high, dusty double-windows. He could see particles floating before the heavy, port-dark curtains.

'Just until Tuesday; I'm having dinner with my cousin tomorrow night, and I said I might see Jodie on Monday. Then it's down to Worthing – again.'

Tony was silent. He didn't want to raise the subject of Anne so early in the conversation.

'I thought we might go shopping this afternoon,' he said, 'I never get a chance to go to the shops, and it's such a nice day.'

'What are you looking for? Anything specific?'

'Well, Rosemary wants a new kettle, but, being Rosemary, she wants a particular type of kettle . . .'

Rosemary was Tony's wife, a smiling, portly girl who

had a reputation for being boisterous and out-spoken. Her conversation was comprised of exclamations and self-referring questions, delivered in a rich Bostonian accent. Her father had once worked in the Kennedy administration – 'a really cool democrat of the golden era'. Rosemary wore thick, burgundy-coloured lipstick, and her black hair was short and glossy. She was sensuous and voluptuous, possessed of boundless energy.

'How is Rosemary? I haven't seen her for ages.'

'You'll see her this evening, if you stay for a drink. She's nearly finished her thesis, and she's teaching.'

Four years earlier, Tony and Rosemary had stayed with John and Anne in Worthing. It had been, John thought, the last happy summer that he and his wife had spent together. For two months the weather was perfect: soaring blue skies above the south downs, the coast basking in the sun from early morning until late evening, the tall white houses of Worthing, Hove and Brighton absorbing the sun as though they faced the Mediterranean. It had been the summer of sunbathing on the roof, and walking up to Chanctonbury Ring in the dusk; larks, like notes of music high above the downs, had pierced the hot air with their song. Anne, dressed in loose white clothes had been relaxed and content; she and Rosemary had played tennis, hilariously, on the beach. John, tanned and healthy, dressed only in voluminous canvas shorts, had dispensed iced drinks. That year, he had worn his hair in a crew-cut; bleached by the sun his blond hair had turned white, and Rosemary had said that he looked Californian. Tony, wearing a panama hat, had lazed in a deck chair hour after hour. The week had passed in a soft, alcoholic daze, coming to an end on a hot blue night when the sea was flat and silver in the moonlight. Tony had sung 'There Goes My Dream' from the roof, and some late walkers had applauded him. It had been an unexpected period of tranquillity and happiness, impossible to sustain or repeat.

After it was over, the weather became chill and changeable; some spell had been broken forever. Anne missed her work and her travels; she said that she felt like an institution, not an individual. She withdrew, and spent many hours in silence. And John, quite suddenly, had not known what to do: he had depended, for the renewal of his charm and his confidence, on Anne's undivided attention.

Anne had said, one afternoon in early autumn: 'It's like, we can't be on holiday forever; and that's what it's like with you – being on holiday, permanently, full-stop. Nothing has any value . . .'

'Is it really that bad?'

'Yes. It is. Because you end up . . . never, quite, happy. . . .'

John touched his wife's elbow, and saw tears in her eyes. He tried to hold her, but she turned away. 'It's of no consequence,' she had said. But it was of consequence, for now the couple had a problem; they lived according to the shape and temper of their problem; it was with them always, wearing them out, demanding attention.

As John listened to Tony in the bar of The Chatham, and smiled at his anecdotes or frowned at his complaints, he felt once more the struggle between his instinct for self-preservation and the onslaught of anxiety. In this light, even Tony's shopping seemed like a cruel reminder of unobtainable normality. John felt that he would give anything, and seek any cure, that would allow him to lose his nervousness and his despair. He longed to forget himself, but sharp shocks, related to his sense of being trapped inside a body that would not allow him to forget or accept that residency, drove him back into his prison of introspection. 'I can't be insane,' he told himself, 'for I'm doing nothing irrational; if I was insane, I wouldn't be having these thoughts . . .' He longed to be outside; he felt claustrophobic. He told himself: 'This too will pass.' And then he thought: 'But what if this is all a dream? What if I'm in a coma of madness and these are just dreams inside my coma?' His palms began to sweat, as he smiled at Tony without listening to him. 'But there's nothing I can do to prove reality is this reality; the dream will answer with another dream. The prosecution will always win . . . It is simply depression,' he concluded; 'four and a half million Americans, and half a million people in England, are taking Prozac . . . That's not counting the people on Lithium, Librium, Valium . . . I'm just one of those . . .' Tony stood up; John, uncertainly, rose to follow him out into the street.

'You know,' said Tony, as the two men left The Chatham, to walk across Hyde Park to Knightsbridge, 'I heard a story the other day about an American psychiatrist who shot one of his patients . . .' He chuckled;

'He said that he was sick of hearing the same bloody problems, day after day . . .'

'But imagine,' said John, feeling hot sunshine on the back of his head, and watching the leaves as they rippled in the warm breeze, 'imagine having to listen to the same thoughts every day, and not be able to put them down; imagine knowing that you are trapped inside, for life, and not being able to live with it . . .' He said this casually, even though the words frightened him.

'Well, you're talking about yourself, aren't you? I can only say, John, that it *will* get better, even though you can't believe that. You're not having an existential crisis, or a nervous breakdown . . . Listen to a professional . . .' He rested his hand on John's shoulder. The friendly gesture seemed strange. He continued: 'Part of what you're experiencing is the side-effects of a strong antidepressant; I know that they call it the 'psycho–active magic bullet', but the bullet's got to find the target. The sensations will become more bearable . . .'

'What if I'm mad?'

'Oh, John – you can spot the crazies the moment they walk in the office. You're not mad.' He paused while John lit a cigarette, surveying the park with his hands in his pockets. John felt comforted, and longed to hold on to his friend. 'In fact,' said Tony, 'you're a bit like your club – you're run down and clinging to a world that doesn't exist anymore. Anne was good for you. Some people are good for one and some aren't. You have to learn to live without her, that's all. What I mean is, most problems can be sorted out by getting rid of dependency on things that are bad for us; you've got to live with losing a thing that was good for you. Note: I said 'a thing', not 'the thing'; it isn't the end of the world . . .'

'She was my life,' said John, lamely.

'But there's more to your life than her; or there ought to be . . .'

John sighed. 'It's like half of me gone, you know? But not forgotten. I simply imagine her new life; I guess its progress in my mind: the job, the flat, the boyfriend . . . I feel it all, and I can't let go.'

'You're full of rage, and depression is suppressed rage – amongst other things . . .' Tony paused. 'That's why there're so many depressives.'

The two friends had reached the edge of the Serpentine; families and couples were strolling beside the dazzling water. John and Tony crossed the grass and made their way towards the avenue of Rotten Row. Traffic glinted in the distance; the trees cast shadows across the caramel-coloured sand of the riding track.

'And you've never worked,' said Tony, eventually; 'That's unhealthy. A lot of people wouldn't have much sympathy for a person who doesn't try . . .'

John nodded. 'I'm not much good at anything,' he said, waiting by the busy road.

'Well, you can help me find this bloody kettle, at least. And then we'll go and get some lunch . . .'

John followed Tony into the crowds of Knightsbridge.

Three

The London clocks had just chimed, from heights of grey warmth; it was a quarter past six. John and Tony were making their way down St Martin's Lane. The afternoon sunshine had given way to a cloudy, humid evening. Now, the traffic and the shoppers were hurrying once more through the matt and muted streets, passing by shops that were closing and restaurants which were about to open, and seeming to ignore the confusion of trans-migration that filled the gap between day and night. London, it seemed, was dressing for dinner – if there was a dinner to go to. It was the time, between six and seven o'clock, when people who had no plan, or no routine or rut to follow, felt at their most aimless and lonely. For those drifters, the hour weighed heavily – 'The cocktail hour,' said Tony, 'is an error posing as a pause' – and any despair increased. The evening was too young to abandon and the day was too old to pursue. For those who had no shopping to take home, no friends to meet, or no lover to court, for those who were neither needed nor wanted, it was a time for fatal introspection, and to study the cheerfulness of others from a centre of stillness which placed the hope of conviviality off bounds. The early lights, of signs and in windows, seemed to beckon the guests of a vast but private frolic – which might not even exist; but the momentum of the busy day had led to this party, and those who were not invited felt their exclusion all the more keenly. With drinks and baths and perfumes, London was preparing to enjoy the night; John White, whose day would end when Tony and Rosemary set off to visit other friends, felt weak and unjustified.

Crossing the road, John watched people greeting one another outside a cinema; their tense features would relax into smiles at the approach of their friends. Sitting at little tables beneath the awning of a café, couples were smiling into one another's eyes, or brooding on the points of an incipient quarrel. Until the last eight months of their marriage, Anne and John had never quarrelled. There had been irritation and argument, but there had also been a generosity which denied peevishness or spite. Usually, the fights had ended in laughter, with compromise won by mixing respect with humour. 'You're useless,' Anne would say, shaking her head; or, 'You knew I was vile when you married me.' John would exclaim, pulling his wife towards him to kiss her. This fondness was the envy of many less suited couples. And the tranquillity of this mutual sympathy had soured so slowly that neither John nor Anne had realised the extent of the gap which was opening up between them. Had they been able to monitor their differences, and grow with them, they might have been saved. As it was, by the time Anne decided to leave, the silence between them was intractable. They confronted one another as though through a web of mistrust and misunderstanding. It was too late, by then, to undo the tangle; the strands of unspoken complaint and argument had become knotted and hard. Neither John nor Anne could understand the other.

'I just can't live like this . . .' Anne had said, eventually.

'Like what?'

'Like . . .' Anne sighed, and gestured angrily at the room around her. 'It's just you and me, absorbing one another. I don't work, we don't do anything; I can't remember what I used to be like.' Anne had sounded as though she was explaining a fact of life.

'Is that my fault?'

'You don't want me to work; so, yes – it is your fault.'

'I have never said that! Work. Go ahead.'

'It isn't just work . . . It's you. I used to think that you were different, now I just think you're lazy.'

But John had never considered that working could be preferable to living one's life through lengthy pleasures and little chores. He had thought that he had simply reached happiness quickly. He began to understand that Anne's dissatisfaction was more acute than he had supposed.

'Let's go away for a while,' he had said, leaning towards his wife.

'I don't want to go away!' shouted Anne; 'I want to get up in the morning, early; I want to dress for work, travel to work, have a point. And . . .' She began to cry.

'And what?'

'And I can't do it with you; it's impossible. I just can't cope with you . . .'

'I'm sorry . . .' John had looked at his wife, and then looked at the floor.

'Oh John,' Anne had said, through her tears, 'I don't even want us to have any children. I just don't want your children.' At that moment, as Anne stared at him as though amazed by her own words, John had felt aware of a lifetime of emptiness; some small thing had turned into a nightmare, some common deficiency had turned mutant, and would now cause havoc. They, Anne and John, had ceased to be normal.

Tony pushed open the heavy glass door of the café where Rosemary was waiting. A sign said 'ouvert' in evergreen italics. The style of the café was dictated by reproduction art nouveau, mirrors, screens, moveable columns and potted palms. The room was long, stretching away beyond a grand piano towards a group of tables set for formal dining. Framed French adverts, for products and drinks which had been discontinued decades ago, hung upon the wall which faced the long, curving bar. The café and its adjoining restaurant were low ceilinged and painted in shades of ivy green and pale yellow. The wooden floor was highly polished, as was the bar, and at regular intervals there stood broad dressers, laden with cutlery, folded napkins and stacked, gleaming ice-buckets. The waiters, who might or might not have been French, hurried about their duties while maintaining loud French conversation, with many shrugs, pouts, and gruff exclamations. In the early evening, the café was half filled, with resting couples, early arrivals, and a few solitary drinkers, who read books and newspapers or watched the coming and going with blank, suspicious eyes. Pots of tea stood on some of the tables, glasses of wine and soda on others. There was a shabbiness about the place, and an air of self-consciousness, which altered the ambience from that of a smart rendezvous to something less – the air of a semi-private thoroughfare, both announcing and defending its privacy. The café smelt of wine, fried fish and cigarettes; the sweeter scent of lilies came from the large flower displays which stood upon the bar.

Rosemary was sitting with her back to the wall, a large mirror behind her, and smoking a cigarette as she flicked through a magazine, wetting her finger to turn the heavy, glossy pages. She had dyed her hair since John last saw her; by the lights of the café it appeared auburn, streaked with blue. She was short-sighted, like her husband, and her brown eyes were made bright and intense by her thick glasses with their frames of imitation tortoise-shell. Rosemary's glasses were round, and she wore them halfway down her short, pretty nose. She looked both business-like and academic, a cross between a young executive and a popular tutor. She was wearing a brown, shapeless dress, black tights, and a pair of thick-soled black shoes. Her mouth was painted with dark lipstick, and her pale face was touched with patches of colour around her cheekbones. Seeing her husband and John, she put down her magazine and smiled, saying nothing. The young men sat down, tired by their walk, and Tony handed over his parcel.

'One kettle, as per illustration,' he said, coolly.

Rosemary glanced in the wrapping of the parcel.

'It's wrapped up,' said Tony.

'I know; I just . . . Where did you get it?'

'That place near Harrods, where you said; for God's sake say it's the right one.'

Rosemary completed her inspection of the parcel and then beamed at Tony.

'It's fine; it's just that there's one with a blue handle, and that would definitely have had to go back. But this is fine, fine . . . How are you, John?'

'I'm fine, thank you . . .' John felt nervous and his palms were sweating. He fingered the bottle of diazepam tablets in his jacket pocket, telling himself he would take 10mg if he grew any worse.

'How long are you in town?' Rosemary waved at a waiter as she asked this question. The waiter paused, and stared impassively at his three customers.

'I'll have a glass of champagne,' said John.

'Make that two,' said Tony.

'I just want another glass of red wine'

'Oh, and an ashtray . . .'

The waiter moved away, shouting the order to the barman.

'I swear to God,' said Rosemary, 'that that guy's not French – and yet they all talk in French; but it's kind of bogus French, like bogus Italian and bogus American. Like this bogus French café. I guess they're selling us something . . .' She paused. 'They're selling us their aura,' she concluded.

John was used to these pronouncements. He smiled,

appreciatively, and waited for the conversation to return to normal lines. He hadn't the energy to assert himself; he had never cared for abstraction. Tony was staring directly ahead of himself, as though he was following some absorbing and complicated transaction. When John glanced over to where he was looking, there was nothing.

'How's your work?' asked John.

Rosemary pulled a face, and sighed. 'Oh, I don't know what to think. Bad, right? I'm revising my thesis for the thousandth time and taking courses in Culture and Consumption for the first year. Oh, and I've got my own little tutorial group . . .'

'Isn't that interesting?'

'It should be, but it's so much reading. You can't blame the kids for being so confused when the department's so at odds with itself, you know? Oh, and a lot of the teachers are shit . . .'

'That's my girl,' said Tony, suddenly rejoining the conversation.

The drinks were brought to the table; John lit a cigarette. He felt hot, and the champagne was so cold that it burned his throat. A party of six young people came into the café, talking and laughing. They had been to see a film. John found their loud conversation, comprised of exclamations, deeply irritating. His instinctive dislike of metropolitan life welled up in him; he imagined Anne in such a group, going along with easy opinion and easy jokes – an admired sophist. His resentment was derived from jealousy; it was like picturing his wife taking part in an orgy. He drank more of his champagne.

'I'm sorry,' Rosemary was saying, 'I was asking how long you're here?'

'Just until Tuesday, or maybe Wednesday. Then it's back down to Worthing.'

'Oh. Are you doing anything nice?'

'Dinner with my cousin tomorrow – '

'Right.'

'And I'll probably see Jodie on Monday . . .'

Rosemary leaned back in her chair. 'Jodie! Jodie Kleist?'

'That's right. She's living in Holland Park, or Notting Hill . . .'

'It's the Notting Hill part of Holland Park,' said Tony.

Rosemary turned to her husband. 'How do you know?'

'We went there for dinner, about three months ago . . .'

'We did?'

'Don't you remember? It was the first time we'd seen inside Jodie's house. There was her, and that Greek girl, and the two boys we didn't like . . .'

'So there was! God! I remember now . . .'

'I haven't seen Jodie for over a year,' said John, 'But she called me up not long ago and told me to get in touch; so I did.'

'You met Jodie through Anne, right?'

The name fell into the conversation like a stone. Tony looked away, and smiled. John coughed. 'Yes,' he said, casually.

'And have you seen Anne?' Rosemary's tone was calm and direct.

'Not really; we spoke on the phone a while ago.'

'Is it all right me talking about this. I mean, it's not as though she's dead or something . . .'

'It's just a looming divorce,' said John, 'and it was my fault, anyway . . .'

'I've told John that he shouldn't think like that,' said Tony, folding his arms. John felt suddenly embarrassed by his friends' attention.

'She just had to live her life,' said John, 'I can see why she left . . .' He reproached himself for reducing his unhappiness to platitudes; he was aware that English people of a certain class and background are conditioned to belittle their emotions when speaking of them, or to speak of them, at least, in the language of a business seminar.

'Was there someone else?' asked Rosemary; 'Is there someone else?'

John looked pensive and shook his head. 'I really don't know,' he said.

The following day, Sunday, was grey. John awoke at dawn, alert and unrested. It seemed unfair that his body had only allowed him three hours sleep. The morning nervousness held him in its grip; each morning he was convinced that his breakdown was finally upon him; with each awakening he felt as though sleep had surely pushed him beyond the limits of recovery. His tired mind, fidgeting from worry to worry, made him question his perception. The thought that all things were external to his senses – sound, light, objects to touch, other people – seemed unbearable; and then there was the fear that he had never really woken up, and that he was seeing, only, the images within his thoughts. He closed his eyes, tight, and then reopened them, trying to convince himself that he was fully conscious. His fear increased. The small room was exactly as he remembered it, but the early light, subdued by thick, mottled cloud, made it look dingy and confined. John could not think of anywhere – any safe environment, as Tony had called it – where he could get some tea: no café would be open, he could not face the walk to The Marriott. He opened a can of Coca-Cola, which he had bought the previous night, and sat beside the window in his underwear, smoking and drinking. He could feel a weight resting on his shoulders, and a tightness around his head. Even the thought of propranolol, beta-blocking his responses, made him feel sick.

The Coca-Cola tasted of warm froth. John's hands and hair felt sticky, picking up his towel and his sponge-bag, he let himself out on to the dark landing and crept downstairs to the shadowy corridor of bathrooms. The bathroom had no windows and was lit by a single yellow bulb, which seemed to sprout from a brass corner bracket. The bath itself was enormous: standing on cast-iron claws, it ran the length of the righthand wall, deep and broad. It was made of enamelled iron, the surface of which was broken by a myriad tiny fractures. Beneath the large taps there was a grey isthmus of discolouration; the black rubber plug, perished about its edges, was secured to a brass chain. As the ancient bath began to fill, the scalding water gave off clouds of steam. John poured in some lavender oil, which filled the room with its pungent scent. He felt as though he was alone in the building, despite having heard a footfall in the passage. The bathroom seemed to have been left unchanged since the 1930s; dim and toneless, it exuded a faintly animal air of masculinity.

Kneeling in the hot water, John stared at his hands, red against his thighs. Then, running his fingers through his hair, he felt warm rivulets running down his back and over his shoulders. 'I shall be clean, at least' he thought. He lay back, submerging his whole body; rising again, he lathered his blond hair with a sachet of shampoo which he had taken months ago from an hotel. Massaging his scalp, and feeling his eyes sting as a trace of soapy water ran across them, he recalled the confused lust which had brought his Saturday night to an end. Now, sensitive with morning, he winced at the thought of his abandonment to memories of sexual happiness. He had also dwelt, with sudden excitement, upon imaginings of his wife's new sexual experiences. The fact that he was ignorant as to her current activities increased his self-torture.

Leaving Tony and Rosemary, he had made his way, slowly and without purpose, through Leicester Square and Soho. The square was busy; brilliant orange and scarlet lights were shining against the buildings; the heads of the crowd seemed like illuminated waves of a night-time sea. High above, two pale spotlights were dancing in the air, endlessly circling one another.

From Leicester Square, John had turned north, making his way up a dark, narrow street which ran between two cinemas; the smells of the Chinese quarter had hit him with full force: an odour of sweetness and decay, of damp sawdust, ginger, cooking and aromatic steam. At Shaftesbury Avenue, beside the fire station, the air had become occidental once more: the smell of petrol and dust, damp buildings, hot fabric and fast food. As the traffic moved on more easily, speeding in the lull of mid-evening towards Piccadilly, London appeared to be breathing more clearly. The cinemas and theatres were full, the gift shops and the tobacco kiosks looked as though they would never close. John had looked into a shop window, where mugs with phallus handles were stacked upon a glass shelf. In the doorway of the shop, studded belts and fingerless gloves were hanging like bunches of blackened seaweed. He had turned away, and headed west.

When the panic attacks had started, John's fear that he was losing his mind had eclipsed the origins of his problem. Anne had become abstract, the inhuman source of a human weakness. After Anne, the structure of John's personality, neglected over the years, had begun to collapse: lost confidence had led to heightened sensitivity, heightened sensitivity had created fear, fear had become dread, dread, despair – and thus the circle was complete, a decline spiral, like a city that loses its economy. 'Everyone,' Anne had said, 'has got their relationship story and their dark secret – it's what new friendships are built on, that first shared confidence . . .' John had hated Anne, for a moment, for reducing his drama to common misery. One October evening, when Anne and he had quarrelled, he had flirted with a girl called Charlotte at the house of some friends. The evening, in recollection, was a humid nightmare. He had been drunk, playing a role: Charlotte, twenty-three years old, boyish and pretty, had responded to his good looks. He had wanted her as a brute indulgence in sensuality; he had wanted her without love, pornographically, and she would probably have gone along with him. Her childish face had leaned towards his, her eyes bright and the smell of wine on her breath; she had been wearing dove-grey velvet shorts over black tights, and a denim jacket. Laughing, she had opened her jacket and pushed out her chest: she was wearing a white t-shirt which bore a red rose and the slogan: 'ENGLAND MADE ME'. Then, John had caught his wife's eye. She was rising from the table with a well-dressed, older man; smiling, she had taken the man's arm.

On the western edge of Soho, John had walked by sex shops and peep shows. He had wondered what it would be like to buy a woman, to ascend a red-lit staircase to some dank sitting-room. The thought repulsed him. As the pavements became darker, and the quietness of Mayfair recommenced, he longed for the slightest encouragement that Anne might still be in love with him. He wanted to feel her warmth and hear her whispers, to be, once more, the sole partner in her amorous inventiveness. At The Chatham, in the dark, he had conjured up obscene images, but found his body unresponsive to their ambivalent allure.

Having bathed, John cleaned his teeth and shaved. He

combed his wet hair back and stared at himself in the small mirror. On Tuesday, he decided, after he had seen his cousin, and Jodie, he would go back to Worthing and try to sleep. He wanted to do nothing but look at the sky, to have, as he was later told, white thoughts in a white room. But he also felt that he needed help. He longed to fall backwards, into some strong arms.

But to whom could John turn? His problems, to his immediate circle of family and friends, were well known; also, the cause of his distress, he believed, was neither unique nor dramatic. His wife had left him, and no amount of advice or sympathy would bring her back. 'The only cure for one passion,' Tony had once cited, 'is another.' This made sense to John, but did not locate his horror. In the crease of his speculations, however wild, was the thought that what Anne had given him, she would now share with others: her laughter, her mannerisms, her memories – even her bouts of ill-temper seemed loveable. And in the midst of his endless circuit around the stations of his love, John dwelt on the notion of Anne finding a new partner. He could almost hear her saying the words, 'my boyfriend', with an absence of emphasis which would prove the new relationship inviolable.

The slow day, slower, it seemed, in the silence of The Chatham, pulled John towards his visit to his cousin's high apartment. He would walk to the Barbican Centre flats in the early evening, finding his way as he went. In the afternoon he lay on the bed and looked through a Sunday newspaper; he saw the words and the pictures, but they didn't hold his attention. He was trying to see his own life, and he felt as though he was rudderless and caught in a current, being dragged to some unknown destination. In London, which demanded that its citizens have a definite direction, his aimlessness was heightened. Anne had been incapable of wasting her time; she was terrified by the thought that time would slip away unfulfilled unless she made an effort to use it. She would always think ahead, planning her movements – her moods, even – in advance, and being disappointed should her days fall short of her hopes. Beyond his self-pity, John could see that Anne, once married, had begun to die of boredom. Marriage had been a great plan, inspired by hope and driven by love, and then, for Anne, it had all fallen short . . . At first, she had not noticed, being much absorbed by novelty and travel; then, settled in Worthing, her smile had wavered as though on the brink of bewilderment. And who could blame her? thought John, now. Disquiet and sadness had followed. Resentment, anger, and the final indifference had concluded the emotional cycle. The process was clear, now, in John's mind; he could see the phases of the marriage as though depicted on a colour chart, marking subtle shades of feeling.

In Madrid, four years earlier, Anne had explained her fear of boredom. They had been walking down a broad, tree-lined boulevard. It was September, and the late afternoon was still hot; the shadows and coolness of evening were hours away; the austere, monumental buildings – the Telephone Exchange like a palace – had looked ancient in the heat, their masonry grey and gold, their windows reflecting a tangerine glare. 'I hate just hanging around,' Anne had said; 'I hate it almost as much as when I was young, and I had to trail around the shops with my parents. It depressed me so much . . . I used to make this chain of associations, without really knowing it, which connected the shops and the grumbling to a sense of death, or something death-like. It was as though nothing could ever matter in that High Street; it was morbid. I hate that British disease: wanting to be at home, indoors, with the curtains closed and tea on the table by five. I don't find that cosy, I find it unbearable. I want grand gestures . . . I don't want to get caught . . .'

Looking back, John realised how little of Anne's speech had actually reached him. Had she given him a meaning-ful look, even then, that he hadn't noticed? He had believed himself, for no good reason, to be immune from her criticism. Now, he did not know what he wanted from his estranged wife. He had taken his strength from her, become co-dependent upon her faith in him, and then . . . He stretched on the bed, wondering where she was, and knowing that he had a phone number which might bring her to him. But the number was six months old; what if she had moved? In any event, he felt that there was nothing she could say which would measure up to the vastness of his pain.

'It's all dead,' he told himself; 'I ought to be bored with thinking about it.' If only his boredom could become greater than his distress. He remembered what Sarah had told him: 'The trick is,' she had said, 'to be okay when everything isn't okay – do you know what I mean?' But John felt scared and anxious, still; something had given way in his mind, and would no longer allow him the retreat of melancholy. He took a propranolol tablet, 40mg, and washed it down with a mouthful of warm grape juice from a silverised bottle. He had to ring Jodie, to see if she was still free to see him the following day. He hoped that she would be.

The sun was coming out over Mayfair; the afternoon was almost warm. Remembering that he could not make out-going calls from his room, he went downstairs to the telephones off the dark hall. On the stairs he met an elderly man, pausing for breath as he clutched the banister with a freckled, bony hand. 'Good gracious me,' the old man said, to neither John nor himself, 'Good gracious me . . .' John, drugged and untidy, almost felt ashamed.

The two club telephones were like broad, heavy-doored wardrobes. They smelt of cigar smoke. Inside each one there was a low shelf, with an old-fashioned telephone upon it, and a straight-backed, leather-seated chair. Calls were charged to each member's account. Once the door was shut, one found oneself in a sealed room, lit by a dim yellow bulb of the kind which glimmered on the landings and in the bathrooms. The light from these bulbs seemed institutional; it was an archaic illumination, reminiscent of prep schools, Whitehall offices, and the corridors and halls of learned societies and university faculties; it was the light of an eternal November evening, confounding the April sunshine which was breaking through outside.

As he dialled Jodie's number, John tried to feel strengthened by the fact that he had not called Anne. He looked upon his silence, now, as a muscle to be built up and toned – a virtual delight in suffering which could make him feel robust, and grimly independent. But he knew that his endurance was fraudulent; for all of his life, his wishes had been indulged, and even encouraged; as other young people had struck out on their own, taking on new places and learning to battle with compromise in order to finally control their own lives, he, it seemed, had lazed in the warmth of The Beaumont, staying at home while others worked. Now, as his doctor described his amorphous, debilitating distress as Agitated Clinical Depression, he respected the shanty shrines of the ritual which offered him a routine to cling to. 'Learning to love my rut,' he would say, thinking of the precise timing of his baths, his pills, the purchase of his newspaper, the exchange of coffee for decaffeinated drinks and orange juice; the mantra of 'I will not phone her . . .' He wanted his rut to be moveable, an apparatus for survival which he could recreate wherever he was; he wanted to fight his horrors by making a safe environment in which everything would always be the same, with no capacity to alarm.

Jodie Kleist was Anne's friend, but she had always liked John. She had once discussed masturbation with him in a way that made him feel insecure. 'Jodie,' he had said, 'never seems quite safe . . .' Anne had laughed at his conformity.

When Jodie answered the phone she sounded out of breath.

'Hello?' she gasped. This greeting was followed by a muffled sound of something breaking. 'Shit.'

'Jodie? It's John.'

'John? John! Hi! I'm sorry . . .' Jodie's voice strayed away from the phone; 'Hold on; I've put you on the speaker . . .'

'Have I called at a bad moment?' John leaned back in his dim, pungent booth and lit a cigarette. Jodie sounded distracted but cheerful, and pleased to hear from him. She spoke quickly, with statements which sounded like questions, and with several digressions. She arrived at her conclusions by complicated diversions, like a person who always reaches their destination late, but by way of interesting, obscure routes. She was thirty-five years old, divorced, and worked as an agent representing four successful photographers. To John, there was something both comic and mystical about these four photographers, commanders of vast salaries, who were never seen but always present. Jodie had met Anne, years earlier, in a Cantonese restaurant in Los Angeles. John had laughed at the exotic location of the meeting. 'Why couldn't you have met in a motorway café?' he had asked, momentarily jealous of his wife's internationalism.

'Because those,' said Jodie, 'are the kind of places where local loners finally snap and go berserk with a hunting rifle . . .'

Jodie came back to the speaker-phone. John could hear her lighting one of the long, thin cigarettes that she smoked.

'I'm just calling,' he said, 'to see if you're still free tomorrow.'

'Of course! I'm looking forward to it.'

'You sound hurried . . .'

Jodie laughed. 'I'm sorry; I've just come in from the garden; I've got the kids this weekend and Arthur's just broken an ashtray and it's all generally . . .'

John could not remember whether Arthur was a dog or a child. He knew that Jodie had both. 'I'll let you get on,' he said. He found Jodie's domestic clamour comforting; it seemed to brighten the heavy atmosphere of The Chatham.

'So you come to me,' Jodie was saying; 'Come at around one, and we'll have a light lunch here . . . Will you have to rush off?'

'I'm not going back until Tuesday, so . . .'

'Well, it'll be good to see you.'

'Absolutely . . .'

His call made, John stood in The Chatham's panelled cloakroom and went through his pockets; he had his keys, cigarettes, wallet and pills. He brushed his jacket with the old, ivory-backed brush which was chained to the side of the full-length mirror. There were rows of lockers and pegs, labelled with small brass numbers. They were empty. An old canvas umbrella was propped up in one corner; a yellowed sheet of fire precautions was neatly pinned to a baize notice-board. It was like a public school changing-room during the holidays. The following day, most of the pegs and lockers would be hidden by coats and scarves and cases; the boys would have returned, leaving their books and their prep – which they were not allowed to take into the dining-room – while they washed their hands and straightened their ties before going in to lunch. There had been a time, before Anne, when the routine of these middle-aged schoolboys had appealed to John. Increasingly, he found their solidity false and their respectability a joke. He let himself out of the club and began to walk east through the mild afternoon. Another day would soon be finished, and that, he thought, was an achievement of sorts.

As he made his way from Mayfair, through the Sunday stillness of Hanover Square, down the last, warm, littered half mile of Oxford Street, to the mansion flats and blackened brick terraces of Holborn, John ceased to be aware, briefly, of the distortions of perception which had been troubling him. He walked slowly, as though caught in a warm, massaging current; plate glass windows, dark hallways, residential railings and locked offices kept pace with his loose stroll. His surroundings, from street to street, seemed to change like a succession of photographic transparencies, clicking off from a slow, automatic carousel. Pale sunshine lapped the curbs and made windows and casements look forlorn. The buildings became higher, and bigger, and less featured: the modern outnumbered the old; the main streets widened, and the sky, too, appeared to expand. The side streets and alleys were empty and obscure; flattened cardboard crates, plastic bakers' trays, and pink rubbish bags, bursting with discarded spreadsheets and ribbons of shredded paper, were piled beside lampposts and heaped against walls. It was the clean rubbish of the central business district, different to the fetid and putrefying effluence of the West End. There was very little traffic and few pedestrians. London, like The Chatham, seemed like an empty school, closed for the holidays.

Passing by a quiet churchyard, a triangle of grass and weathered tombs, hemmed in by sandstone houses with white windowframes and low roofs, John paused in his journey to sit down. He found a long wooden seat, lay back and lit a cigarette – his twentieth of the day, he noted. Spring had freshened the trees and flowers; clumps of yellow crocuses looked cheerful against the white stone of a grave. The season was poised to change, holding back for a last ecstatic week before the flourish of summer. A couple came into the churchyard through a railinged entrance on its far side: they had their arms about one another's waists. John watched them from his bench. He had become fascinated by couples: he would catch himself following them through the subways of underground stations, and through the richly scented halls of department stores. Alternately envious and sad, he would study the way that hand would find hand, or head rest on shoulder; he would try to catch inflections of language and imagine himself in love with someone new. But he could never see the face of this new love. He esteemed Anne's temperament too much to believe that she could be bettered, or replaced. He thought of the question in those terms.

The couple walked on; John leaned forward with his

head in his hands. He could not cry but his body seemed to tremble with sadness. He heard Anne's voice in his memory: 'You fuck other women and you treat me like shit . . .'

It had been the final blaze of rage; the last moment of dialogue before Anne had slipped away from his orbit as soundlessly and swiftly as a retreating planet. Their mansion had broken and it had been John's fault; his current despair was the shameful charge for too much laziness and confusion. Pressing his fists into his eyes, he murmured 'My girl, my girl . . .' When he finally looked up, blinking, at the conifers and lilac of the small City churchyard, Anne seemed more distant than ever.

Sarah Vick had become anxious about her informal supper party. Her friend April would now be arriving on her own, because her partner, Roger, had left her for another woman. The relationship had been recent and far from settled, but for April, who believed herself to be unlucky in love, the separation was both painful and symbolic. 'I just get too intense,' she had said on the telephone to Robert, who had conveyed the news of the altered circumstances to Sarah in silently mouthed phrases, as she was chopping basil for a salad.

'But we'd love to see you, on your own,' he had said, warmly; 'Sarah's cousin will be here, so there'll just be the four of us . . .'

A few minutes later, Robert had found Sarah rummaging angrily in the fridge, her composure temporarily disturbed. 'There's going to be us,' she said, staring crossly at a head of celery, 'and two emotional invalids . . . Oh Robert, it's going to be hard work and it was meant to be nice . . .'

Robert stood with his hands in his pockets and stared out of the kitchen window.

'I liked Roger,' he said, finally.

'Yes. He seemed quite nice . . .'

'What did he do? I know that April told us.'

'Supply Teacher. Bermondsey.'

Robert nodded, and began to gnaw at a large olive.

April was the first to arrive. She was dressed in black and clutching a bottle of wine which was wrapped in bright green paper. The evening was still light, but heavy clouds were building over south London, visible from the Barbican tower. April's hair was long and straight, the colour of teak but streaked with grey. Her face was finely featured but she believed that her nose was too sharp and her mouth too thin; a light, barely noticeable moustache of blonde down ran across her upper lip. Her eyes were brown and kindly beneath her slightly angled eyebrows. She was tall, and conscious of her height; she crossed rooms with her shoulders slightly hunched, but always sat with her back very straight and her hands resting in her lap. Born and raised in Canada, she had lived in London since she was sixteen years old. She worked for an American trade journal. She hoped to get an overseas posting, the more so now that Roger had gone. She talked quickly, and without self-consciousness, about her ambitions and her problems. Nibbling unsalted cashew nuts, she sat in the broad leather armchair and talked to Sarah while Robert mixed a salad dressing. A glass of amber coloured wine was placed at her feet; a long American cigarette was smouldering in the ashtray by her elbow.

'Yep,' she said, with feigned objectivity, 'there are dumpers and there are dumpees . . . And I'm down the dumper . . .' she added wryly.

Sarah nodded, sympathetically.

'I mean, God . . .' continued April, sipping her wine and picking up her cigarette, 'I've got to the age when I've got enough to worry about . . . I worry about every grey hair, wrinkle and headline; I worry about those little mole things you ought to have removed; I worry about being too old to have children and then I worry that I wouldn't want children anyway. Some chance. I have six books about assertiveness and stress, and I can't find the time to finish any of them . . .' She paused, tossing a nut into her mouth. 'And then, just when I think that I've met someone really nice, who's going to be a bit, you know, supportive, the bastard runs off because "he's not equal to the responsibility of a mature relationship . . ." Fuck him.'

Robert came out of the kitchen, and sat down quietly with his glass of wine. He felt sorry for April but said nothing; she was defining her problem. This, he believed, was April's part of the evening: the thirty minutes or so in which she could feel quite free to speak solely about herself. Robert and Sarah were good listeners: Robert often felt that their role as confessors, umpires, or champions of their friends' relationships did much to strengthen their own. At night, in bed, they would sometimes discuss the lives of their friends before finally going to sleep; their books would be put to one side, and their hands would touch above the cool material of the duvet cover. With the lamps out, the London night would fill their window with blue and orange light. Then they would feel safe and happy to be together – all the while acknowledging the frailty of their little raft as it negotiated the choppy waters of early middle age. Then April's voice recalled him to the pale modern sitting-room.

'But I made him,' she was saying, 'I mean, he had no confidence when we met, not really. He was just a guy in a tweed jacket with a crap car, trying to get over his first marriage . . .'

'That was June?' asked Sarah, quietly.

'Right. Good joke, huh? June – April . . . Anyway, all I did, it seems, was give him the confidence to fall in love with somebody else. For months I kept the compliments and endearments pouring out, telling him how great he was, and how he ought to be nice to himself, and for what?' April's eyes grew pink around their edges and began to water. Robert studied his glass of wine and Sarah said: 'It doesn't matter; go ahead.'

'I mean, shit . . . It's like either I feel sorry for someone and can't bring myself to leave them or I work really, really hard to keep myself detached, and cut off my emotions, only to get walked over . . .' She paused. 'God, I feel sick . . .' A tear ran down her cheek, cutting a glistening path through her pale powder. 'Oh, shit . . .'

84

Robert discreetly spat an olive stone into his palm, and Sarah fetched April a tissue.

'You're better off without him . . .' said Sarah, 'I mean, if it simply makes you sad.'

April nodded, and, excusing herself, went into the bathroom.

John White, meanwhile, was making his way across the raised concrete walkway which spanned the Barbican water-gardens. The subways and pillared squares were deserted; the light was soft and grey, as though drawn from a medieval cloister. The residential towers soared up into the heavy evening sky; a milk-coloured glow reflected off the highest windows. The dusk was quiet, save for the musical splashing of a small fountain. On the further side of the water, John could see a woman tending to a terracotta bowl of geraniums, vigorously turning the dark soil with her trowel. She did not look up, and did not see him. Just as he reached the entrance to Sarah and Robert's staircase, he felt warm rain. He stopped, and listened to the gentle drops as they pattered against expensive windows. He felt tired.

The evening passed quietly, with salad and pasta and shared opinions. John and April were politely friendly to one another, but each forgot the other within minutes of leaving the apartment. Later, Sarah said to Robert: 'I think that went quite well, don't you?'

Four

'I've only read two books that changed my life,' said Jodie, '*The Wind In The Willows* and my husband's diary . . .'

Jodie Kleist was sitting cross-legged in an ornate armchair which faced the tall windows of her drawing-room. Her copper-coloured hair was piled up on her head and held in place by two ivory sticks which were carved with blue and scarlet hieroglyphics. Behind her, massed in pale profusions were slender embroidered cushions, which gave her seat the appearance of an imperial throne. This regality was borne out by her bearing. She was dressed in tapering brown trousers, which finished just above her ankles, and a white silk shirt which she wore untucked and buttoned up to the neck. She was barefoot and her toenails were painted with gold polish. Her features were both maternal and bohemian, a mingling of expressions which gave her cheerfulness an edge of cynicism and her gentleness a strain of inscrutability. She was thirty-nine years old, and she seemed to those who knew her to be equally relaxed on a variety of social levels. She was said to have had a turbulent past, in which drugs, aristocrats, rock music and modern art had all played their parts. It was also said that she knew everybody: that was her label. But she laughed at this reputation, as though the past, however colourful, was of no interest to her and all that mattered were the photographers whom she represented and the society – volatile and complex – which had formed around her. She was neither a working mother nor an apologist for a generation; she scarcely mentioned her children and often said that there was nothing worse than an old friend. It was difficult to guess her wealth, just as it was difficult to guess her age. She finished her sentence, staring into the bright windows, 'In fact, I didn't really start to read until after my divorce . . .'

The room looked out on to a long, overgrown city garden, just minutes from Notting Hill tube station. It was filled with a submarine light, the colour of green water. The walls were papered with pale green silk and the windows hung with rolls of spotless white cotton, blocked with oblongs of afternoon sunshine. Squat steel candelabra, dripping with pendants of mauve glass, stood at either end of the inlaid table and the high white mantelpiece. Above the mantelpiece there was a broad mirror, set in a frame of lilac-coloured wood, and this reflected a Mexican tapestry which occupied the greater part of the facing wall. The tapestry was coarsely woven, depicting an angular, saffron-coloured city set against a bone white background and bordered with pink and emerald patterns. To one side of this, a high, glass-fronted bookcase, with elegantly curved doors, dark with age, revealed the mixed spines of old and new books. A low, circular table, bearing a lamp of painted steel sun-flowers, and a skull, stood before a long, high-backed sofa, strewn with garish cushions which were embroidered with silk paroquets and tropical sunsets. The exotic clutter seemed endless, presenting an effect like that of a Victorian library transplanted in North Africa. Every wall and surface was covered with pictures, keep-sakes, photographs and antiques. Framed advertisements, dating from the 1920s, for Egyptian cigarettes and French tonics, were hung beside still-life paintings of fruit on ebony, and a child's drawing of a blue yacht. There were thick, perfumed candles, sticks of incense bound with pink ribbons, in thick clumps, and a painting on wooden planks, blasted by a small-bore shotgun. It was a room contrived to overwhelm the eye, asserting the tastes and history of its owner with assured, intoxicating stylishness. Many of the objects and artefacts told stories from Jodie's life: there was an Indian shawl, stitched with moonstones, which she had worn when she saw The Rolling Stones in Hyde Park; two sketches by Jim Dine, inscribed to Jodie by the artist, hung in an alcove; there was a leather jacket with the words ENGLAND'S DREAMING painted crudely upon its back, draped over a powder-pink chaise-longue.

Anne had found Jodie's taste delightful; she had never tired of admiring her eclectic collection of treasures and ephemera. To John, the rooms were too rich and too confused; he found them cramped and depressing. But the whole of Jodie's four-storeyed house, from it's dark, Gothic hall, to its bright, restful attic rooms, maintained her heady style. The staircase was lined with books and paintings; even the bathrooms were lit by beaded lamps, and decorated with tribal art and Christian icons. There was a second drawing-room, far grander than the first, on the second floor, and this held marble busts, an allegorical painting, potted palm trees and a full-sized harp. When Jodie held parties, well spoken local girls, chosen for their beauty and their manners, stood by the doors with silver salvers laden with spiced (some said drugged) hors-d'oeuvres and triangles of smoked salmon. Further up the house, the childrens' bedrooms were filled with wooden toys, books and miniature furniture; the windows of these higher rooms looked out into the branches of two lime trees, which brushed the front of the house.

Jodie and John had lunched in the sunny, barn-like kitchen. A vase of white lilies dominated the table, incongruous and stately beside the bowl of hardened brown sugar and the plastic bottle of semi-skimmed milk from the supermarket. They had eaten a salad, with cherry tomatoes, sweet herrings, quails' eggs and a mild, rubbery cheese. Jodie loved hot pickles and mustards, and complemented the meal with curried chutneys and aromatic dressings. Afterwards, they had eaten stewed pears with cream and cinammon. In the drawing-room Jodie served bitter coffee in small Algerian cups, before sitting to face John in her throne-like chair. An ashtray of green crystal was placed on the floor between them. Cheerful and blasé, Jodie led the conversation, weaving her discourse with ease and adding strands of detail and colour by finding something obscure or alarming in nearly every subject. And yet, to John, she did not seem quite real; she did not deal in facts, but shied away from information to revel in concepts, anecdotes and abstraction. She was charming, but unnerving.

'The thing about therapy,' she said, 'is the controlled nervous breakdown . . .'

'I just thought that it might help,' said John, feeling provincial.

'But do you really need sorting out, do you? I mean, you're not insane . . .' Jodie stressed this word in a deep voice, widening her eyes. 'And I'll bet that you don't do one irrational thing, all the live-long day . . .' This phrase was almost sung. John thought yet again that Jodie's affections shattered like mercury when pinned down.

'It's just this anxiety thing; it's really frightening – it colours everything . . .'

'Are you taking pills?'

'Diazepam, propranolol, Prozac . . .'

'The Holy Trinity . . . So you're Prozacked? I mean, now?'

'Second month.'

Jodie leaned forward and tipped the ash off her cigarette into the saucer of her coffee. For a moment, John thought that she was going to kiss him.

'Have you noticed,' she said, 'how everyone, these days, wants to get well? It's like we're all sick, a whole lot of us – or we think that we are. People used to talk in financial metaphors, and now they use the language of illness, treatment and recovery, all the time . . . It's weird, really. How did we all become so ill?'

'I don't know. I haven't really thought about it . . .'

'That's because sick rooms cause self-obsession . . .

But I do remember, when I first met you, thinking: there goes the sanest man in England.'

John could not tell whether or not Jodie was teasing him. He felt almost offended, as though she was belittling the days and nights of fear which he had endured. He looked over at a small white table, no wider than a dinner-plate, which was inlaid with mother-of-pearl. Five .303 bullets were arranged in a white dish upon it.

'You must be a dozing depressive,' said Jodie, 'and something set you off . . .'

'Have you ever been in therapy?'

'For the last twelve years . . .'

'I don't mean to be rude, but, shouldn't it have worked by now?'

'I don't know what you mean.'

John felt like Alice, addressing the caterpillar in Wonderland.

'I suppose what I mean is, do you feel better?'

'Yes. In some ways. But there we go again: "better", "well" . . .'

John found Jodie's attitude unhealthy; it seemed to verge on occultism, or some abstract, mystical, creed. He wanted to talk about precise symptoms, and specific drugs.

'A lot of it's what my body tells me – my body screaming out, you know?'

John lit a cigarette, and realised that he felt sleepy. He wanted Jodie to realise that his distress had become greater than the source of his distress.

'Perhaps you're just bored,' said Jodie; 'I mean, now

that Anne isn't there and you've got all this time for morbid . . . sick talk . . .'

John rubbed the back of his head. Jodie's expression was sympathetic, and encouraging.

'It isn't quite as simple as that . . .' he began.

'She's seeing someone else.' said Jodie, in a firm voice; 'Anne is seeing someone else and I think it's pretty serious.'

John took a sudden intake of breath, leaned forward, and closed his eyes. He felt Jodie's hand, resting lightly on his shoulder.

'Never mind,' she was saying, 'It's not the end of the world . . .'

It occurred to John, as he raised his head and saw Jodie's eyes from margins of fading darkness, that his life had been irreversibly altered. His conception of himself, for so long, had been dependent upon the hope that Anne still cared for him enough – in a diluted manner of how he cared, at least – for their old dialogue to be resumed. That had been the thimble upon which he had balanced the anvil of his days. Now, at Jodie's few brutal words, he understood the futility of his redecorating, in preparation for Anne's return, of the house of love. While he had tried, he believed, to adjust the past and hone the present, in order to make his wife comfortable once more, Anne, blameless, empowered by a new lease of life, had been elsewhere. Her indifference towards her estranged husband was now complete. She was never coming home.

'Who's the man?' he asked, quietly.

'Does that matter?'

'At the moment,' John faltered, 'it seems to . . .'

'Some guy where she works, I think.'

John nodded. 'Well. That would appear to be that.'

'Hadn't you guessed? I mean, it has been a while since you split up.'

'But I didn't split up,' said John, with sudden exasperation, 'She left.'

He paused. Jodie smiled.

'Here's a question for you,' he went on, 'What do you do with love that isn't wanted?'

'Get over it – like flu; throw it out – like anything past its sell-by date.'

A low chime was heard. 'That's the door; excuse me for a minute.'

'I should leave, anyway.'

'No, you don't have to. Sit!' Jodie patted John's shoulder and went into the dark hall. John heard the heavy door being opened, the gentle sound of muted traffic, and a low exchange of greetings. Then, Jodie's brief, infectious laugh rang out, and there was the sound of a heavy parcel placed on the floor. John stood up and stared at the empty fireplace; the thought that Anne was seeing someone else, that she would maybe, that evening, be lying in someone else's bed, or twisting her earring as some other man talked to her, was unbearable. He felt lightheaded, as though he was using strength which he no longer possessed.

'John?' Jodie was calling to him; he could hear her clear

voice. But he was recalling his infidelity to Anne; his one act of betrayal, despite his love, committed in the dusk of marriage. However he looked at it, he felt, it was sordid and shabby.

'Oh, John . . .' Jodie's voice sounded once more from the hall, and then the low voices resumed.

The girl had been a house-guest, the younger sister of one of Anne's friends; Worthing in winter had mirrored the silence and ill-temper of the frozen marriage. Anne and her friend had gone out, early one Saturday afternoon; evergreen fairy-lights had been at odds with the sluggish sea. Anne had not looked at her husband as she was leaving.

'When will you be back?' he had asked.

'Later.'

The girl had been bored, recently thrown over . . .

'John! Will you please give me a hand with this box . . . John?' Jodie padded barefoot down the hall and beckoned to her guest.

'I'm sorry,' said John, 'How can I help?'

He followed Jodie back into the hall. He didn't notice, at first, the person standing to one side, their figure dappled by the crimson and blue light which fell through the stained-glass panels in the front door.

'This is Rachel,' said Jodie, as John was pulling the tape-bound cardboard crate down the hall; it was heavy. 'Rachel's been helping out Archie, who's one of my clients . . .' John nodded, and looked up briefly. He couldn't make out Rachel's face.

'Hello,' a voice murmured.

94

But John, his task completed, had made his goodbyes and turned to leave. He felt embarrassed and rude, but he wanted to leave Jodie's house. Soon, he was walking up the sunny hill, thinking about Anne, but thinking more about himself.

The following day, as he had planned, John returned to Worthing. Six weeks passed. The precocious spring turned wet once more; nature seemed swollen with water. The lilac hung heavy, its purple and white cones weighed down with moisture; the vivid new leaves and the young grass were battered and flattened by the rain. The damp days had a greenish hue, softened in diminished light; the pale-petalled roses which were coming into flower looked like luminous notes of music, dispersed across a moss-coloured score. The sea was flat, steel grey, retreating at low tide to reveal acres of salty, rippled sand, cut by shallow streams and tepid, colourless pools. The wind was erratic and mild, sometimes fresh and blustery, otherwise warm and oppressive. As the season advanced, with deepening greenery and lengthening days, the weather became humid. It was like a tropical spring, refusing to settle or loosen its hold, stifling summer . . .

Finally, the first hot days broke through a fissure in the low white sky. The town came to life in brilliant sunshine; the promenade was amber in the sunset; the quiet, sea-facing houses exchanged their air of emptiness for an atmosphere of mild awakening, their lawns newly mown and their neat blinds half lowered. On the two blocks of flats, just three years old, the weathered windows were cleaned and polished. The shops and arcades teemed with life – young teenagers on skateboards and bicycles rehearsed casual stunts in the square beyond the precinct; widowers and elderly couples walked slowly from shop to shop; youth and old age pursued their different, yet equally fixed, routines. Sometimes in the evenings a warm sea mist would roll in, drifting through the trees and moistening the flint-encrusted garden walls. Then the air would smell of damp and salt and earth, a scent which seemed to raise people's spirits and make them think of the future.

The chasm into which John assumed that Jodie had dropped him was not as deep as he supposed. The bulk of his grieving over Anne, it seemed, had been done. At first he had expected that his latest shock, inspiring rage and jealousy, would extend his nervous depression and add a further term to the sentence of entombment which he had endured. But his anger and his fear had now been localised: a portion of his dread had sharpened into pure jealousy, the tinder of this emotion having been stored for so long, and having become so dry, that it swiftly and fiercely blazed into nothingness. There were some nights, but fewer dawns, when he lay awake in his empty house, or sat in the silent drawing-room, facing the feeble promenade lights, and spoke to Anne in his mind. Then, with mounting rage, he would offer impassioned defences of his own behaviour and accuse his absent wife of cruelty and neglect, selfishness and deceit. Throughout these tirades, he would become convinced that his reasoning was correct, and his arguments fully justified. He even thought of telephoning Anne, and on one occasion let the call connect, but did not allow the answering tone to ring.

To defend himself, John created his own routine: sometimes it was called his rut, and other times his ritual, but it was essentially a timetable for survival. In this manner he tried to tame the moods which had controlled him. When this worked, he felt as though he was taking a mood-stabliliser, such as lithium. His fear did not fade, but it became sedimentary, sinking to the floor of his days and allowing other time to clear. Like a person recovering from a long illness, who leaves their sick room after several months, he rediscovered his surroundings and saw them by the brighter, clearer light of a new season. Prozac, as an anti-depressant, was now established within his system; its side-effects, from insomnia to nausea to anxiety were less troubling. Daily, the little grey and green pill was taken with a cup of sweet Chinese tea, early in the evening. John's mornings remained short tunnels of fear, threatening collapse, but there was now some arsenal of defences – a corresponding index of answers to the litany of doubts and horrors which had taunted him with their ceaseless, terrifying questions. His dependence upon other drugs began to lessen: propranolol could be relied upon to ease physical symptoms of anxiety, and diazepam remained his friend and his minder – his Little John – to be called upon when the fight seemed overwhelming. Diazepam could still the world, bringing sleep and soothing indifference; it became talismanic, and John, to his surprise, would fetishise his prescribed drugs as though to love their role in his life.

He still questioned, however, the manner of cocoon in which he was surviving; chemicals, curiously elongated emotions and the changing weather seemed to vary the tone of his days. He became heliotropic, requiring and turning to the sun; on hot days he sat on the roof or balcony of his house, renewing his tan as he dozed through the afternoons. The rest of the time was spent in learning to love his rut.

He would waken, now, at seven o'clock in the morning. The early sunlight no longer distressed him, for he had allowed for that fear within his routine. Wrapped in a towel, he would go down to the kitchen and make himself a strong cup of Indian tea. This was a bad time of the day. The kitchen was at the back of the house, on the lower-ground floor; it had a door which let out on to a small garden, filled with herbs and flowers, and surrounded by a fence which was overgrown with honeysuckle and mock orange. There was no lawn, but a concrete patio. The kitchen appliances were modern, with white cupboards above green-tiled work-surfaces; three windows, covered by grey Venetian blinds, looked out on to the garden. The kitchen was an annex of the ground floor dining-room, which was tiled with charcoal coloured marble. There was a long wooden table in the dining-room, the top of which was painted pale pink. The walls were white, and two extravagant plaster statuettes stood on either side of the white-pillared fireplace. An iron-framed mirror hung above the fireplace, facing a tall, hand-painted canvas screen, which depicted three angels with violet wings, holding hands over a placcid sea. This had been made by one of Anne's friends. The dining-room had once been the hall, and a low flight of steps led down from its furthest corner to the front door.

Having made his tea, John returned to the bedroom where he had formerly slept with Anne. This was on the second floor of the tall, terraced house, and it had french windows which opened on to a tiny upper balcony. There was just room on the balcony for a small wrought-iron table and a slatted metal seat. Opening the windows, John would sit at Anne's old dressing-table, and smoke his first cigarette of the day. For some reason, he always opened one of the dressing-table drawers, and rested his hand inside it as he sat there. The coast road would still be quiet, the sea calm. As he drank his tea, John would try to study the horizon of his day with clear eyes, and envisage the hours in manageable sections.

The next event in the routine was a long bath. John would first collect his mail from the hall – which would have arrived while he was smoking – and then make himself a second cup of tea. He would take his tea and post to the bathroom, placing the mail on the window-sill between two bottles of ivory-coloured gel. He placed his tea on a narrow circular table which was edged with brightly coloured shells. Then he would clean his teeth. He favoured a clear green toothpaste, pumped from a linear dispenser. The citric scent of morning bath oil would mingle with the steam of the running bath. Cooling the bath with cold water, John then weighed himself, noting any variation at all on his usual twelve stone three pounds. Throwing aside his towel, he would then lower himself gently into the bath, kneeling first to get used to the temperature of the water. Sluggish with the new warmth, he would stare for some minutes at the bathroom wall, not thinking; then, he would splash his face with water prior to washing his upper body with a heavily soaped sponge. All of these actions were carried out, every day, in precisely the same order; he could no longer imagine starting his day in any other way. In the past, with Anne, there had always been some sound in the house; now there was silence. John liked to think that he could recreate his rut anywhere, and carry its comfort with him.

Leaning back, John stretched out and allowed the hot water to trickle over his head and shoulders; he inhaled the bath oil, hungrily. Then, to combat any incipient nervousness, he would distract himself (Tony had called it, laughing, a displacement therapy) by reading his mail. This, too, was incorporated into John's rut: he would always begin with his bank and credit card statements, which were as predictable as his weight. His capital allowed him a modest monthly budget, which he seldom overran; the small mortgage, which he now paid alone, was direct debited from the building society; his domestic bills seemed to be growing smaller. The magazines and advertisements would come next, their columns of information and images soothing his nerves. Any personal letters – which were rare – were saved as a treat. 'I don't seem to have many friends,' he would think, sometimes.

He also shaved in the bath, propping a small black mirror against the wall, and massaging his face with an eucalyptus shaving oil. As he shaved, and renewed the connection between his actions and his body, he would find himself slowly reviving; on good days, his confidence, at this point, would beget confidence. It was a great improvement on the trembling, drugged, trips to the twenty-four-hour coffee shop at The Marriott Hotel. Finally, he would shower his hair, rinsing the bath when he had finished. Wrapped in a towel, he would return to his bedroom to dress. Each stage of this process had its own character, and the familiarity of these characters was a comfort.

There was very little left in the house to remind John of Anne: her clothes and her books had been collected by her saddened parents, three weeks after their daughter had left. All that remained were objects which the couple had bought together, and the scent of French perfume, which lingered in the drawers and wardrobe in the bedroom. The perfume was sweet and sharp, a concession to slight freakishness, which, practised by Anne, was transmuted into subtle glamour. Conventional by instinct, Anne's few deviations into the exotic were emphasised and intensified by their rarity: she had worn men's suits, in her time, complete with tailored shirt and silk tie; she had dyed her hair the colour of claret, for six months, and once went to a dinner party with an Hell's Angels tattoo painted on her upper arm. One night she had come to bed dressed in the cheapest and briefest of black and scarlet lace underwear; 'I felt like buying some tarty underwear,' she said, 'so I did . . .' These occasional aberrations had roused John's admiration; now they returned to haunt him and he forced himself to dismiss them as manipulative and uninteresting. He was learning to dislike his former wife.

In the first floor drawing-room, propped up on the mantelpiece, there was a brightly coloured calendar depicting Saint Bernadette, which Anne and John had bought in Lourdes. The calendar was out of date, now, but the couple had found its kitsch exotic; it remained on the mantelpiece, between a blue vase and a carved block of sandalwood. The young Saint was gazing up at Mary with brimming, innocent eyes; in certain lights The Virgin's blue sash became luminous and furrowed, like creased satin. Little ornaments such as this, which brought back so many memories, were difficult to throw away. John wished that he could bring himself to put all the keep-sakes in a sturdy cardboard crate, and store them in a cupboard. Instead, he incorporated the cleaning and tidying of the house into his rut and his routine; dusting and vacuuming, washing windows and cleaning the bathroom, were all good therapy. He became neurotically tidy.

By the middle of the morning, John was ready to go out. His previous laziness and reliance upon others to organise his day had given way to a certain order and assertiveness. It was almost as though he was trying to make up to Anne for his earlier complacency – not that she cares, now, he thought. It was becoming warm enough to walk along the sea-front, and enjoy the sun on one's arms and face; the empty sea sparkled; except at weekends the promenade was quiet. John would walk to the centre of Worthing – away from the fenced-off site of his father's old hotel; retirement flats were being built on the land where The Beaumont had stood. The demolition had taken place the previous autumn; John had watched, curious but unmoved, as the white walls of his childhood home were torn apart like cardboard. The front down, and the valuable fittings salvaged, the hotel had looked like an opened dolls' house; strips of faded wall-paper flapped in the wind. The rubble and noise were the source of John's income – his exemption from work. The new retirement homes were small and neat, with gardens and patios which seemed to fit together like pieces of a children's jigsaw puzzle.

Having bought his newspaper, John would cross over the coast road and visit the bright new supermarket. Here, life was centred; a bad day was when the supermarket seemed alien and strange. Making his way up and down the aisles, following a precise route from the colourful drifts of fruit and vegetables, past the brilliant white fridges, beyond the wines and spirits and on, slowly but surely to the bakery and check-outs, John would feel secure in the comforting environment. It was like being well again; he had noticed that many people's problems seem to fade in the supermarket. He bought himself treats: children's cereal, four-packs of flavoured drinking yoghurt, kettle chips and cheddar cheese smoked over apple wood. His only sadness was remembering the loneliness of shopping without Anne. There had been days, shortly after the separation, when John woke to believe that the marriage could be saved. On mornings such as those he would clean and tidy the house, almost feeling cheerful, and place vases of Anne's favourite flowers in the sad and empty rooms. Then he would go out and do the shopping, attaching to each purchase a small narrative which he thought would amuse or touch his wife. Returning home, he would plan in what order the items should be displayed for their anecdotal magic to bring about the reunion which had seemed, in the early morning, almost within reach. But then, as he sat in the quiet kitchen, surrounded by packages and bags, with the clock above the fridge ticking loudly, he would realise that Anne was not coming home, his hope had been a delusion, and his shopping was just bags and products. Those had been bad days, but far worse had followed: anger and despair, once refined into a new concentrate, had delivered fear and led to clinics and drugs and hopeless telephone conversations. There had been days when he had not even recognised his home. Now, shopping on the bright May mornings, John clung to his routine as an escape from confusion and terror. He scolded himself for his weakness and anxiety; he compared his suffering to that of nameless others, whose situations were far worse. He believed that he had changed.

John's way home was through the new precinct; this ran beyond the Regency terrace to one side of the square, and down a back street which ran parallel to the sea. Here, old shops mingled with new; outfitters and sweet shops, their decor undisturbed since the 1950s, stood side by side with record shops and jeans shops, where young teenagers gathered outside. The sea was always close; the sky became deep blue by noon; the wind was often hot and fierce. On fine, calm days John ate his snack lunch and drank his fruit juice sitting on the little balcony of his house. There was a long lawn in front of the terrace, running its length; geraniums made a pink border: the scene looked like an old coloured postcard, which had been left to fade in the sun.

One day, towards the middle of May, John heard a voice calling up to him. Looking down, he saw that it was Jodie. She was shading her eyes with one hand and waving.

'John? Are you there?'

Jodie was wearing blue jeans and a white shirt; a cream-coloured pullover was knotted over her shoulders; her dark glasses had jet-black lenses, set in narrow frames. She looked like a young county mother.

'Jodie?' John peered over the balcony, 'Hi . . .'

'Hi . . .'

'Hold on, I'll throw down the keys.' He was pleased to have some company; as he was making his way downstairs, he found pleasure in the fact that he had just bought some freshly-ground decaffeinated coffee, which he would be able to share with his guest. He heard the front door opening; Jodie met him in the sparsely furnished dining-room and kissed him on both cheeks.

'I hope we're not disturbing you;' she said, 'it's such a glorious day and I had to drop some stuff off in Brighton and pick up some other stuff . . . God, I sound like a drug dealer; my stuff, in fact, is a picture frame from a friend; then I collected a jacket which I found months ago, and was having altered . . .' She looked around the neat, quiet room. 'It seems completely different,' she said, 'although it's basically the same . . .'

'Yes.'

'It's a lot like life, I suppose . . .' She took a step back: 'But you look really well! You've gone blond again . . . Much better than when I last saw you.'

John picked up his packet of cigarettes from a large painted bowl; 'Let me get you a drink,' he offered, 'what would you like?'

'Actually, I said that if you were here we'd meet Rachel; she's just parking the car. She came down with me – well, drove us, really . . .'

'Rachel?'

'You ignored her at my place . . .'

'It was a bad day; I'm sorry.' John paused and then decided to ask the question he was longing to ask: 'Have you heard from Anne?'

'A few weeks ago, yes.'

'How is she? Did she ask about me?'

'She's fine – but we didn't talk about you . . . Hey,' Jodie had picked up the melted stump of a perfumed candle, and was sniffing it, 'I want one of these.' The candle had not been lit for months. 'She's going to Greece.' She concluded.

'With anyone?'

John wished he did not care; his feelings towards Anne

had become abstract, but her name and her memory brought with them unhappiness and jealousy, like the name of a particular city can be eclipsed, immediately it is mentioned, by a sudden sense of animosity or depression. These feelings, for John, had become worn out by excessive consideration; his periods of depression had shortened; he clung to shrines of his ritual and the route of his rut.

'I honestly don't know if she's going with anyone,' said Jodie, 'and you should try not to care. What is it that they say, these days: "Get a life?", "Have an attitude?" It used to be money attitudes — "Go for it!" and now it's recovery attitudes.' She gave a short, slightly mocking laugh, which made her seem strong and admirable.

There was a light knock on the front door.

'It's open,' shouted Jodie. 'That'll be Rachel, come to dig us out . . .'

John's interest was suddenly roused; he had no recollection of Rachel at all. He waited for Jodie's friend to make her way up the shallow flight of stairs. Jodie watched him, a smile playing about her lips. She raised her eyebrows. 'Big meeting,' she said.

The figure who emerged, self-consciously, to stand on the edge of an oblong of sunshine, looked ill at ease and embarrassed. John had been expecting — he did not know why — that Rachel would be tall, blonde, loose-limbed and relaxed. But the young woman who was facing him, with her head turned slightly to one side, to keep the sun out of her eyes, was slender and awkward. She was less tall than Jodie, but more compact than petite. She had the air of a person who was merely dropping by, and whose personality had been left elsewhere, in a place that she cared about but would not impose on others. She was dressed in black, slightly shabby clothes: a long black jacket, flared at the waist like a skirt, reached down to just above her knees. The buttons on this jacket were flat and round, and covered with black cloth; the upper half of the collar was finished in dark blue velvet. Beneath this, Rachel was wearing a black T-shirt with a low scooped neck. A black velvet choker encircled her slender neck. She was small-breasted and lightly tanned. Her trousers were black and narrow, stopping at her ankles, and on her small feet she was wearing scuffed black Chelsea boots, extremely pointed. But her jacket was clearly expensive, contrasting with her plain trousers and boots. Her hands were soft and brown, with delicate fingers; the backs of her wrists revealed a pale network of blue veins.

'John,' said Rachel, displaying the newcomer like a lot in an auction, 'this is Rachel; Rachel, this is John.'

The couple shook hands briefly; John was aware of a cool palm and a light pressure. A sweet, fresh perfume passed before his face. Yet there was a moment, as the two strangers greeted one another, when John looked at Rachel and experienced a moment of weakness; he felt for a second that he was going to faint, as though a heady atmosphere which he had been enjoying had suddenly made him light-headed. This was a sensation which he could just remember from his adolescence; he redis- covered the feeling with as much shock as surprise. It pierced him, with tantalising potency, like a ribbon of scent inhaled on the street that evaporates before one can place it. Then there was a sense, similar to that of dropping between floors in an express lift: it was alarming, yet pleasurable, a momentary loss of centre and solidity. This was accompanied by an internal warmth, like that of fear or nervousness, but caused by a chance encounter with a glimpsed expression or scene which one hopes will repeat the emotions it has provoked. Such a feeling, and such an image, could only be chanced upon: it presented itself fully formed and inviolable; it triumphed in the instant, requiring no further qualification or conditions. John had once read, somewhere, that everyone discovers one face, once, that is their ideal. One would not necessarily get to meet the owner of that face: some people spend their lives searching for its nearest equivalent. The term used, albeit weakly, to describe this discovery would be love at first sight. And John's shock corresponded to all of the clichés which he had formerly associated with that notion of instant, complete love: he had not been anticipating any emotional disturbance that morning; he was wholly unprepared for the sudden aesthetic tremor which had run through his senses, sweeping all before it. At first, he assumed that he had simply imagined, through some trick of the light or angle of impression, that he had found a face he could never tire of watching – that he would defend with his life; surely, he reasoned, when he next looked at Rachel she would appear quite ordinary? Anne's features had worked upon him slowly, in pace with her conversation and attitudes;

this new sensation was like an assault. He turned to Jodie, offering his guests coffee without listening to his words.

'That would be nice,' said Jodie, leaning against one of the dining-room chairs and looking through her bag for her cigarettes. She still had not taken off her dark glasses.

'We can have it upstairs,' called John from the kitchen. He could not bring himself to look at Rachel again, in case he had been mistaken. He was trembling, and his mind was blank as he made the coffee. His guests ascended the stairs with a mixture of apprehension and curiosity. John suddenly worried that he was forcing his hospitality upon them.

'Would you sooner go out?' he called.

'Make the damn coffee . . .' called back Jodie, in suave, abbreviated tones.

John waited for the kettle to boil, suddenly aware that Anne, for a few moments, had ceased to be the sundial that he turned to when he wanted to know the time in his life. He carried the tray up to the drawing-room, treading carefully. He found his guests standing on the balcony, looking out at the placid, whiteish sea.

'Hot weather goes straight to my stomach,' Jodie was saying, 'I mean, Thailand made me really sick . . .'

Rachel, as John put down the tray, turned to lean against the balcony balustrade; resting her weight on her elbows, with her narrow shoulders slightly hunched, she looked back into the drawing-room with an expression which was inscrutable but not hostile. Her face was lowered, and she raised her eyes to look at her host. She smiled – politely, John felt. But pouring the coffee he told himself that he had not been mistaken: Rachel had a beauty, for him, of which he could never tire; sweetness, wisdom and gravity were mingled in her features; with every turn, John believed, and with each new falling of light and shadow, he would find new beauty to admire. Or, rather, he would lose himself wholly in the contemplation of her features. And with each stolen glance he felt the certainty of his discovery increasing. In ten minutes, he believed, he had fallen unconditionally and utterly in love.

'Can we help?' Jodie came back into the room with her dark glasses pushed up on her forehead.

'No; it's fine; sit down anywhere . . .'

Jodie sat down in an armchair, crossing her long legs. 'This room is quite dark,' she said, looking at the moss-coloured walls and the heavy, pale canvas drapes. There was a long deep sofa, upholstered in a broadly striped material of crimson and silver; before that, on a low table, there was a carved African box and and a cast-iron ashtray.

'The rug's lovely, though,' she added, 'and the mirror . . .'

All three looked up at the large mirror, with its extravagantly wrought gilt frame.

'It just seems like everyone's got one . . .' said John.

He offered cigarettes; Jodie shook her head, but Rachel, sitting far back in one corner of the deep sofa, took out a packet of French untipped cigarettes.

'Do you mind if I smoke these?' she asked, in such a quiet voice that John had to lean forward to hear her.

Jodie was talking about London, her friends, and her plans for a garden party. She invited John but he was only half-attending; he was watching Rachel as she lit her cigarette: looking down, she frowned as she inhaled, her eyes watering slightly with the blue, pungent smoke. She looked as though she was slightly angry with the cigarette, and John's heart went out to her in her struggle. Once more, he studied her face, irresistably drawn: her features were poised on the brink of seriousness; it was as though the remnants of her youth had frozen, at a particular moment of happiness, to retain a teenage freshness whilst allowing new marks of maturity. Her mouth was a soft bow of light brown, glistening faintly with the lustre of a dull copper lipstick; when she smiled, and her lips widened, there seemed to be a breadth to her expression which implied that she wanted to be more relaxed than she could permit herself. Her chin was slightly squared, and when she turned the shadow of her jaw and neck presented a delicate profile which was also strong and clear. The plains of her cheeks were childlike in their smoothness, but bars of subtle colour raised her cheekbones to adult angles. Her nose was small and straight, her nostrils slightly broad; but all the sweetness and clarity in her face, to John, led to the glory of her eyes. Rachel's eyes were dark brown – so dark as to be almost black; they were sad yet enigmatic, their expression alternately soft and withdrawn. Long black eyelashes curved out to precise hemispheres, the lashes on her lower eyelids perfectly separated and defined. Rachel's eyes appeared to be resisting and studying the outside world – to John it seemed as though they were posing some question or offering some challenge which he and Rachel knew about, but were yet to articulate. Her brown hair was shaved at the back, but loosely cropped on top. It was a cleverly messy style; tousled yet severe, revealing small ears and a calm, tanned brow, Rachel's hair was both scruffy and glamorous. This, to John, completed the young woman's beauty. All he knew, as Jodie talked, and he replied, and Rachel listened in silence, was that he wanted to know everything about the young woman, dressed in black, whose perfume smelt of new-mown hay and damp flowers.

Five

'I was born in 1969,' said Rachel, 'the year The Velvet Underground released their third LP. I never went to college. My mother died when I was twelve and I loved her more than anyone. I never knew my father.'

Mid-December; six months, for John, had flowed invisibly, like a fast current beneath calm water. His routine – his rut which he clung to and used to soothe his fear of open-ended time – was now held in place by Prozac, the bullet-shaped capsules of which had the functional anonymity of office furniture. His ritual of taking this antidepressant, with a cup of sweet tea in the afternoon, was a routine within his routine, or, as he thought, a rut within his rut. The rut, which had evolved as a means of surviving the passage of time, was now a benign structure which doubled as a temporal calculator into which all fear could be fed. 'But it's still kind of neurotic,' Rosemary had said. The rut was a daily timetable, from waking to sleep, which meant that John would never have to make a decision, if he didn't want to; 'If I'm afraid,' he thought, 'I'll know that it's time to buy a newspaper, or have a sleep, or make a telephone call.' Even the scalding rumours of Anne's new life, which sometimes reached John when he was least prepared for them, could be allotted their place in the rut. When he dared to test his confidence by deviating from his rut, John fell back on the thought of drugs.

'Opinions differ,' Tony had said, 'I say that Prozac is a good drug . . .'

'There's a new joke in the States,' Rosemary had added, licking a bead of red wine off her finger, 'What's the fifty-first state? Answer: Prozac! I sort of imagine Prozac to be one of those dry, square, dusty states, somewhere in the middle. The Christian fundamentalists say that it's the devil's drug – did you read that thing in *Toxic Psychiatry*? And there's another book, too . . .'

John had read the other book. He had developed an interest in the chemical control of his condition. Researching Prozac and thinking about Rachel had all found their place in the rut. But now that Rachel was sitting opposite him, in the green and gold dimness of the Chatham dining-room, he was thinking more of his struggle to find her. They were alone together for the first time. Rachel was watching him; her eyes were as dark as coal, with tiny silver filaments of light in their centre. She had told him that she wore contact lenses; she owned lenses in different shades; this evening her lenses were jet black, making one unsettling disc of each pupil and iris. People stared when they caught her eye. John was enthralled by the play of shadows across her face, which rose to beat gently against her features from the twin gold tears of the candles. She leaned back in her chair, with its ornate frame of gold painted wood and its worn cushioning of emerald green velvet. She dabbed the corner of her eye. 'They need their drops,' she said.

As the nights had grown shorter, John had fallen to sleep with the thought of Rachel walking by his side, her arm slipped through his, the toes of her black boots scuffed and dusty as they had been when he first saw her. He had thought of the Haymarket in the ceaseless rain, and of a different London, brought to life by Rachel. Questioning Jodie, he had been told, merely, 'Oh, Rachel's a friend; you should call her. She'd like that.' And she had given John a London telephone number where Rachel might be reached. She had sounded neither curious nor amused at his interest; in Jodie's society, John thought, attraction was not treated with furtive embarrassment. Loosely, absurdly, but with a slight thrill, he had conjectured that Jodie's friends enjoyed an openness which was based on an alternative morality. But still he was embarrassed. He called the number once, and listened to it ringing; he tried to picture the room to which his call was being connected. It could have been a white, sunny studio, or an office, a dim-balconied council flat or a house in the suburbs. The phone rang on – the sound of an empty house. He had thought of Rachel walking to her phone; she walked with a slight, awkward swagger, and she blinked heavily, widening her eyes as though to refocus them. She had mannerisms which made her seem vulnerable yet proud.

He had tried again a few days later, finding his excuse in Jodie's invitation to her garden party. This might justify his enquiries. Rachel had sounded surprised to hear from him. 'I hadn't thought of going. I wouldn't really know anyone there.'

John had blushed. 'What's the party for?' he had asked, tracing a line along the telephone with his thumb-nail.

'I think it's something to do with the summer solstice – she has one in winter, too . . .'

'Oh, really?'

'Or it's just Jodie. You know, she loves entertaining.'

Was Rachel bored? 'It would be nice to see you again;' John spoke in measured tones, 'maybe if I'm going to be in London we could meet . . .' He had been afraid that this clumsy phrase might disgrace him in Rachel's eyes.

'I'm a bit busy for the next couple of weeks – but if you're coming up anyway call me nearer the time. I don't mean to be . . .'

'It's okay; I'll try to call you when I know . . .'

John had clung to this shred of hope, telling himself that he didn't care even though he thought of Rachel daily; she was beside him, invisibly; she cast an influence over his daily routine like a household god. Panic lessened, but there were still long days when John's palms were wet with nervous sweat; he would be horribly aware of the physiological constitution of his being; he would fear the reality of his eyes, skull and tongue. The thought of being alive – a thing of nerves and tissue – disturbed him. 'The millepede tripping over its own legs,' Robert, Sarah's boyfriend, had remarked.

'My mother was a speed-freak,' Rachel continued. 'She took amphetamines and heroin. She was twenty when she had me and thirty-two when she died. Jodie knew her quite well, in fact. She had a freak's funeral – a wake I suppose. There were all these people I'd never seen before, stoned and chanting . . .' She paused, resting her fork on her plate; the club's crest could be seen, scratched and faded, beneath furrows of white sauce. 'They all brought loads of orange flowers.' Rachel's black dress was sleeveless. Her flared jacket – black with a velvet collar – was thrown down beside her chair. A waiter had tried to move it, but she had stopped him. The black dress was short and tight; Rachel wore black tights and black Chelsea boots which showed off her long, slender legs and the curve of her hips. Her velvet choker was replaced by a black chiffon scarf, its knot reversed and the ends hanging loose between her shoulder-blades. Her cropped hair was roughly spiked and scraped back over her ears; the twisted points glinted with grease. Her lipstick was dull gold, which made her lower lip look soft and full. A heavy silver bracelet of beaten square links had slipped down her arm, bronzed by candlelight.

'My mother was very beautiful, she said. 'She'd been a model when models were skinny and had big baby eyes. She liked to say that she'd modelled for Bailey and had a bit part in *Blow Up*, but it wasn't true. She only worked when she felt like it.' Rachel sipped her wine. 'Her parents were well-off, middle-class people from the suburbs. Her father had been in the Army. I mean, she wasn't Edie Sedgwick but she was young, pretty and not particularly conventional. She loved clothes . . .'

John had not gone to Jodie's summer party. Thinking of it, he had pictured a stick of ochre-coloured incense, trailing twin blue plumes of scented smoke into the warm summer air of the garden. He had stuck to his rut. Then, as the dead heat of the eighth month had lifted, and the mornings became fresh, bright and damp he had called Rachel once more. She had sounded irritable; he had listened to her footsteps echoing over bare boards as she walked with her phone from one room to another. 'It's not you,' she had said, 'it's just stuff.' He had suggested that they meet for afternoon tea. Politely, she had refused.

With the autumn, John's thoughts of Anne hurt less; the open cut had become a bruise. He had spoken to Robert and Sarah about this, when they came to visit him in Worthing. The day had been clear and blustery; they had stopped for tea in the old arcade. 'It's like it's all gone at once,' he had said, watching Robert blow gently on his cup of tea; 'I thought that I'd remember bits, but now it all seems unreal. I found a photograph the other day — it must have been taken ages ago, when she was in Australia. She'd just got out of the pool on the roof of a hotel; she's got dark glasses on and she's laughing into the camera: it was like she was a stranger. She looked completely new — without my memories of her. I was quite shocked.'

Sarah had nodded. When she listened, she looked into his eyes, not blinking.

'But the worst thing was, I didn't mind anymore; I felt something, but I couldn't recognise the sadness . . . And then I thought, what if I can't be sad or happy anymore?'

'Could it be the pills?' Robert had asked.

'Maybe.'

John had wanted to say that he had fallen in love, but superstition stopped him. Rachel was made rare by secrecy.

'April thought that you were nice,' Sarah had said. This was untrue. 'But I don't think that you're for April . . .'

'What's she doing now?' asked John.

Robert sighed. 'She's into reflexology and vitamin C. She says that C is the best vitamin.'

'And she's just come back from Canada,' added Sarah.

Throughout the autumn, John was roused by the freshening days; the scent of the season and its quick chill inspired him. He called Rachel twice: the first time she had been in a hurry and had promised to return his call. When she didn't he called her again and invited her to Worthing, for lunch. Once more, she refused. Then, in the third week of November, Rachel had telephone John.

'Jodie's ill,' she had said.

'What's the trouble?' John's tone was light and cheerful.

'They think it might be cancer. She's been having tests, and . . .' Rachel's voice was clear and even; 'They know it's cancer.' she said, finally.

John's brightness had died away like the sudden blaze of a bonfire. The fear that he had become trapped inside a dream brushed his thoughts.

'She may get better,' Rachel went on, 'but she won't talk about it. She's so angry . . .'

'Is she in hospital?'

'No. I mean, it's so sudden. Almost overnight. She's actually planning a trip to Finland, for the New Year . . .' Rachel spoke without sadness; but, John thought later, she was speaking without doubt . . . He did not know Jodie well enough, he felt, to feel the full shock of the news.

'And will she still be having her winter party?' Gusts of rain were buffeting against the kitchen windows. John was sitting at the empty dining-room table, his radio-phone cradled beneath his chin. The room was growing dark. 'I'm coming to London next week,' he said, suddenly, before Rachel could answer his question. Jodie slipped out of the conversation, neither ignored nor forgotten but momentarily put to one side.

'Where do you stay?'

'In Mayfair, at my club.'

'You mean, like a gentlemen's club? Like the Reform Club or something?'

'It's a place called The Chatham; it's nothing like as grand as The Reform. It's more like an old hotel . . .' Then John remembered Jodie's illness and his voice lowered. 'So that's what I'm doing.' He glanced at the souvenir from the shrine of Saint Bernadette; as usual, he didn't know whether or not he believed in miracles.

'Do they let women in?' Rachel asked.

'Only on Friday evenings, for dinner. Why? Would you like to come?'

'I'd find it really interesting.'

They had agreed to meet the following Friday. Rachel would come to The Chatham Club, on Ladies Night.

John looked at Rachel. Once more he was drawn to a beauty which he felt he could never tire of watching; it stilled him and enthralled him, as though each inflection of the woman's expression and movements was a pledge of future happiness. The dining-room, lit by candles and heavily shaded lamps, smelt of hot wax and perfume. Rachel was relaxed, but there was secrecy in her bearing. She was friendly but humourless, open yet defensive; she accepted courtesy and politeness – the formal deference shown by men to women at The Chatham – without questioning or gratitude. In this indifference, thought John, lay an irreversible loathing of the club as an institution. Her movements were modest, her sexuality was revealed, it seemed, on trust. John was weak before her. His nerves had been on edge since early evening.

To reach the bar of The Chatham one crossed a pallid and cheerless anteroom. Green leather benches lined the walls and an electric chandelier cast a bright, unflattering light. On Friday evenings this outer room was always busy, crowded with chattering men and women who bore themselves as though they were attending a smart wedding. They had to speak loudly to make themselves heard. It was like the undulating clamour of the drinks interval at a big theatre. Groups and couples were crammed together, seldom mingling, and new arrivals had to push their way through the throng in search of friends or somewhere to sit down. The Chatham bar, usually, seemed spacious and grand, a sudden crescendo of shabby magnificence; its panelling was dark with age and smoke; its moulded ceiling, high and remote, gave the room a church-like air. Deep armchairs, the leather of their massive cushions worn through to cracks of pinkish suede, were grouped in pairs beside small, circular tables. On each table there was a small hand-bell, to call the steward, and a brass-shaded lamp. These lamps made broken wedges of bronze-coloured light, which glinted off the black ridges of the marble fireplace while leaving the remainder of the long room in shadowy darkness. The room responded best to winter nights, when sunshine and daylight could not reveal the faded decor and battered furniture.

John had found a seat beside the ancient double doors which were open between the anteroom and the bar. Looking around, he had found it difficult to believe that he would soon be meeting Rachel. She was due to arrive at eight o'clock. While he waited, he saw faces that he recognised, but nobody said, 'What can I get for you?' or slapped his shoulder in greeting. 'All these people', he thought, 'seem to have one mind and character; they don't seem like individuals at all.' His palms were still damp and perfumed from splashing his face with cologne. Rachel had been late. Eight o'clock had struck and many of the members and their guests had gone upstairs to dine. They made their way slowly, ascending the elegant curve of the central staircase with a soft, assured tread to the dining-room beyond. Some of them raised their eyes to admire the painted ceilings, high above the stairwell. John had been about to order a second drink when the club porter, a parody of aged loyalty, had approached him.

'Mr White?'

'Yes?'

'There is a Miss Denis for you, waiting . . .'

Rachel had been standing in the gloomy, marble-tiled hall; she looked as though she had chosen the least conspicuous place, at the foot of the dark staircase which led to the club's bedrooms. When she saw John, she smiled briefly, but her face did not relax with her smile. John shook her hand beneath the impassive gaze of the porter. 'Come through,' he had said, 'let me get you a drink . . .' The porter had returned, stern-faced, to his feebly lit desk. He had performed his traditional duty of ensuring that no lady was left on the premises without a recognised escort.

The bar was quieter; Rachel had taken a seat in one of the dim alcoves. She had seemed uninterested in her surroundings. Blackened Victorian portraits of minor statesman and public officials hung down from the obscurity of the high ceiling. Rachel had asked for a glass of whisky. The line of her eyebrows was angled and precise, her eyelashes were individually defined by strokes of powdery mascara. John saw that there was no playfulness in her character, coy nervousness or generosity. John had hoped that conversation would be easy. He wondered whether her reticence and stiffness were evidence of a hard, practical attitude towards life and a lack of imagination. Her perfume was the same as she had worn in Worthing, the green scent of a wet summer garden; she smoked a French cigarette with watering eyes.

Their table was set away from the centre of the room, beneath the tall arch of a window. The dining-room was the most impressive room in the club; its ceiling was painted with gods, garlands, piled clouds and sunbursts. The walls were pale green, the floor polished parquet. The tables glinted with silver and glass, trembling on heavy white linen; waiters in green livery scurried between the kitchens and the diners. Through the window one could see the still, cold street, with a light burning orange on the far side. After her second glass of wine – John drank water – Rachel had started to talk, telling the story of her life in statements of fact, like a printed biography. There seemed to be a lapse of time between her words and her appearance, a pause for potential which John found overwhelming, like the slow pulling out of a wave. She ate only vegetables in white sauce, cheese and fruit. Having come up to dinner late, they watched the grand room emptying of its crowd of guests.

'I was at school the day my mother died,' said Rachel, 'The school was in Shepherd's Bush – we lived in Hammersmith. It was called a progressive school because there was lots of art and drama, but I always felt awkward there, like I was somehow unclean. I suppose I was a late developer. I couldn't join in with anything, and these other kids who'd been told that they were great actors or brilliant artists or something used to make me feel like a servant. I had no confidence, so I spent all my free time with my mother. She always played with me; and she discussed things with me like you would with an adult. She'd given up drugs but her heart was weak. We used to make clothes and dress up in them; we'd pretend to be two princesses, held prisoner in a castle.'

John had been away when his father had died, but he

had known that death was near. He felt sorry for Rachel, and for the younger Rachel whom he could picture in his mind's eye – a subdued little girl standing on the edge of the playground, always walking alone . . . Rachel's brow looked pale and calm between the dark spikes of her fringe and the angles of her black eyebrows. Her contact lenses seemed to hold the candlelight. 'Both of my parents are dead,' said John, 'and you always want to see them again, whatever . . .'

Rachel looked at her folded napkin; the club crest was embroidered in silver thread in one corner of the white linen. 'Whatever . . .' she repeated; when she moved her body shifted gracefully within her clothes. John longed to see her naked, stretched out, open to him. The image was distant and forceful.

'When my mother died,' Rachel said, 'I was taken to her parents' house, out in the suburbs. I went to a new school in Croydon, but I hated it. I felt as though I'd lived one life already and I became withdrawn. My grand-parents were kind to me, but I couldn't face another family home. It all seemed wrong, transitory . . . They'd buy me lovely things and make a fuss of me, but it was like I couldn't wake up. I felt trapped inside myself, like I was buried alive. I couldn't wait to leave school and leave home. I thought that if I could just get back to London, everything would be all right . . .' Rachel paused. 'I didn't have any friend,' she said, slowly, 'but the woman who lived next door, who was quite young, used to take me shopping with her. When I was fourteen she took me to Brighton for the day, just the two of us.

That was such a vivid day; I had this impression of endless summer, and endless freedom. And the thing was, when we got back, I cried and cried – because I'd been so happy. Jill was terrified that my grandparents would think she'd upset me, which she had, in a way . . .'

The dining-room was nearly empty. The head waiter was flicking through bills with his wetted finger and counting under his breath. John remembered how Anne had always told interesting stories – it had been her trademark. She had travelled widely and found herself in comic or unusual situations, which she described well. He remembered how angry he had been when someone had remarked, not knowing he could hear, 'The thing about Anne is that she's a little too interesting, if you know what I mean . . .' Rachel had no anecdotes; her mystery was internal, like a secret which John was longing to share.

'How will you get home?' asked John, 'Do you have far to travel?'

'I live near Liverpool Street.' said Rachel, 'Have I talked too much?'

'No. It's interesting . . .' John wanted Rachel to stay; he was afraid that he'd been rude. He had noticed how Rachel would place limits on certain subjects, or answer certain questions, with the phrase 'Just is.' This expression was like a full stop which doubled as opaque explanation; it countered analysis or discussion; it closed an issue for good. The mystery was sealed in different ways, so John had to wait for his questions to be answered in Rachel's own way. His world had shrunk to the table where Rachel sat facing him. She had dined well, making no comment about the food; she was content to talk but she asked few questions. Her voice was low, accentless and confident.

'Where's the women's loo?' she asked, rising. John told her and she crossed the long room towards the top of the curving staircase. She walked with her head bowed and her hands by her sides, her wrists loose. John watched her, entranced by the sway of her hips. The mansion in Hill Street had once been a private house; a Victorian surgeon had left it to his friends and colleagues, so they could carry on with their dinners and discussions after his death. A committee had been formed, new friends were made – rooms were set aside for provincial doctors to have a London address. The grandeur had survived for a hundred years or so; it was unlikely that the club would survive for another hundred . . . To John, the place grew darker and less substantial with each of his visits; it was like an extravagant setting for a glass jewel – almost unwearable. When Rachel returned she smiled as she sat down. John wanted the evening to go on for ever.

'I left school as soon as possible, straight after my sixteenth birthday,' she said; 'I got a job in the West End, working on a perfume counter in a big store. I'd always loved Oxford Street because it seemed so alive.'

'Did you enjoy it?'

'It was marvellous, at first. It was better than being a

secretary or something. I didn't have any qualifications or anything . . .' She lit a cigarette.

'Exams and ambition are things that don't matter if you're not used to them. All of your friends are probably overeducated as a matter of course . . .'

'But you seem . . .'

'I don't mean to be rude; there's nothing wrong with education. I'm just saying that I didn't have much.' Rachel brushed her cheek with her thumb-nail. John noticed that her thumb-nails were painted black. 'What did you do then?' he asked.

'I was ill for about two years, in and out of hospital. I'd been living in a house with one of Jodie's friends and her husband, in Battersea, but then I had to go back to Surrey for a while.'

John wondered what the illness had been; he thought of Anne's home and their visits to see her parents. It all seemed years ago. But before he could gather his thoughts, Rachel had started speaking again. He butted in, 'My wife was from Battersea.'

'I know.'

John looked surprised.

'Jodie told me.'

What else had Jodie told Rachel? 'We could have our coffee in the library,' said John, 'nobody ever goes in there.'

The couple went downstairs, passing the door to the smoky bar. At the foot of the stairs there were cabinets filled with china figurines: an orchestra of monkeys, some transluscent cups and saucers. The library was empty; its three long windows were covered with velvet curtains, loosely sashed. The room was low-ceilinged; in its centre there was an oval table, with magazines and the day's papers laid out like cards in a game of Patience. The walls were lined with glass-fronted bookcases; the book bindings gleamed dully in the low light. Some portraits and a cartoon drawn on a napkin hung in the two small alcoves. The wide fireplace, where an elderly gas fire was burning with a loud hiss, seemed dwarfed by the broad marble mantelpiece, carved with columns and bearded satyrs. On the tiled hearth, to the left and right, there were ebony statuettes of turbaned negroes holding flaming torches. A carriage clock maintained its portentous ticking in the middle of the mantelpiece; above this, a gilt-framed mirror, reflecting orange darkness. Rachel sat down in the corner of the long leather sofa, her legs curled beneath her. Her perfume mingled with the dry smell of musty books and threadbare carpet. John sat at the other end of the sofa. 'My friends would like you,' he said, 'Am I keeping you?'

Rachel blushed, suddenly. 'I'll go soon; Jodie says that I talk too much.'

'You obviously got better – after you were ill . . .' said John. 'And then?'

'Then I met this man called Simon . . .' The words seemed out of character; John could not imagine Rachel being close to anyone. The thought saddened him and thrilled him: he tried to picture someone's arms about her, or domestic laughter. It was suddenly unbelievable that Rachel had a past.

'Simon lived near here, actually,' said Rachel, 'He had a flat in Curzon Street. It was really cramped inside, even though there was a porter and fresh flowers in the lobby; the windows were metal-framed and the kitchen was too small to wash up in. It reminded me of a hospital . . .'

'What did Simon do?'

'He was a lost soul, I suppose. He'd been in the Army, and then he worked as a vintner's agent. But, when I met him . . . I couldn't drive, I hadn't got a flat, or a job – I seemed incapable of making any money . . .'

'Where did you meet him?'

Rachel dipped a cube of brown sugar in her coffee and felt its rough edge with her tongue. 'At a party,' she said, absently. 'But Simon was strong, in some ways . . .' She said this as though John had suggested otherwise. 'He was always giving instructions and warnings: "You do it *this* way, Rachel," or "The thing about making a proper salad dressing, Rachel," – there was a proper way to do everything, for Simon, from making scrambled eggs to cleaning a swimming pool – and he knew all of them. It was incredibly comforting, like having a strong shoulder – a pad of hard muscle – to rest my head against in bed . . .'

John swallowed and lit a cigarette; he longed to capture Rachel's interest. When do I speak? he thought.

Rachel went on: 'And yet when Simon was asleep – this vast, assured, repository of knowledge – he looked so childlike and vulnerable. There was always this serious expression on his face as he plodded around in his dreams, showing people how to do things . . . He knew how to plan his time, you see; duties and treats were correctly proportioned within his efficient days . . . His days were his kingdom, in fact: he ruled them, and they served him like subjects.'

Just like Anne, thought John.

'And then he went to France; he wanted to find himself, he said. I was heartbroken at the time. He was much older than me, though, and I suppose I knew that he wouldn't stay forever.'

'When did you split up?'

'Oh, more than two years ago, now . . .'

A muffled farewell sounded from the hall; John and Rachel heard the heavy front door creak shut; but nobody came into the library to disturb them and they sat in silence for a moment.

'It's funny how confident people are often lost souls,' said Rachel, 'Only you don't find out for a while.'

In the darkness, John blinked; he was out of his depth. The simple evening, spliced in his mind to simple romance, had become complex; it was no longer working to rules which he understood. 'You talk beautifully,' he said.

Rachel did not answer. Her posture stiffened and she folded her hands in her lap. John wanted to kiss her; he felt a need, stronger than any he had ever experienced, to touch her soft mouth, dusted with gold, with his own. He had always been confident in his dealings with women – affectionately ridiculed by his friends for his amorous successes. He had kissed other girls, before he was married, without doubting the seam of welcome which would be buried beneath the surface of their response. As a student he had attracted many women with ease, so used to his own appeal that his self-assurance would become infectious. Those women who had not liked him – and there were many who loathed him, instinctively – had called him immature and dull. Anne had been a challenge; Anne, with a mixture of pride and pleasure, had once described him as dangerous. But with Rachel, John felt neutered and powerless. He adored her but could not communicate his adoration.

'One day last year,' he said, 'I woke up and I was only aware of my head . . .' He paused, unsure of his words. 'It was the most frightening thing I've ever known; and the thing is, now, even when I'm really happy, I remember this terrible fear. It's like something went wrong in my head, and I'll never be able to be happy again . . . Because of this thing . . .'

Rachel's expression didn't flicker. 'And the thing is?' she asked.

'I have this feeling; it trips me up when I least expect it – I remember it and it's there. It's like the fairy story about the man who would find buried treasure provided he didn't think of a white dove while he was digging . . . Only with me there's no treasure; the treasure would be to feel safe again. It's like I'm trapped inside my head, that everything I am – what I think of as me, my consciousness – is just a small, smothered light locked inside this bone container that I carry around on my neck. There's only two small holes . . .' – he pointed at his eyes – 'to see through. Like prison windows . . .' He paused, 'I don't know why I'm telling you this; a few years ago I'd probably have tried to impress you, or seduce you, and now I just want to feel well again. But the thing is, I'm right – on one level; physically, we're all just trapped thoughts – even our bodies are outside of ourselves . . .'

'I know what it's like to feel trapped,' said Rachel, suddenly, 'I lived with that for ages – you wish that you could tear your body open, and let your self out . . . You've just got to find a way of living with it; if you can do that, then you'll forget about it, and you won't be able to remember the feeling.'

'Oh – it's better than it was,' said John. 'And I'm trying to sort it out. But how did you forget about it? Or haven't you?'

'After Simon, I went and worked as a volunteer, in the infirmary at Lourdes . . .'

'Oh, we . . .'

'I know; I saw the picture of Saint Bernadette in your house.'

'It's a peculiar place,' John did not mention how Anne and he had bought candles and trinkets from the souvenir shops because they found them colourful and funny.

'It's a cross between a carnival and a cancer ward,' said Rachel, 'Except for the shrine itself. Unless you're a Catholic, you've just got to think – well, if it makes them happy . . .'

'Are you a Catholic?' asked John.

Rachel looked surprised. 'Me? God, no.'

'What did you do? Just turn up?'

'I heard about it from a priest who came to the hospital I was in; he was nice, like a priest out of a film – so I went. Just for a month.'

John wondered whether Rachel was telling the truth. 'It's true,' she said, smiling.

'Is it interesting?'

'It is if you like talking to people; I can't speak any other languages, but you pick up bits of French, Spanish, Italian . . .'

'What did you have to do?'

'Just help in the hospital – stuff like that.'

'But wasn't it depressing?'

'People dying is always depressing. But I went back, at Christmas. It's not an intellectual thing; I'm sure it's selfish of me, in fact.'

'All those lost souls,' said John.

'Anything but lost; whatever you might think, those people believe in something when they come to the shrine. They're not lost.'

'But doesn't it raise their hopes unfairly? Doesn't it make people believe in miracles?'

Rachel stubbed out her cigarette. 'But they believe in miracles already. That doesn't mean that they expect to get one – of their very own . . .'

John was impressed. 'Anyway,' Rachel concluded. 'I don't know anything about the religious angle. That's just what I did. I'm sorry you haven't found a way to forget your stuff – to get better . . .'

John sat still, stroking his eyebrow with his finger. It was after two, and the club was silent once more. 'I'm

sorry that I went on about myself,' he said, 'You'll probably never come back . . .'

'Oh, Jodie had already told me – that's why I agreed
to see you.'

John was curious. 'What had she told you?'

'About you being ill, and the drugs . . .' She stood up
and brushed the front of her black dress. She put her
hands on her hips as John reached over for her coat.

'We haven't talked about Jodie,' he said, 'Do you think
she'll get better?'

'I don't know. She's ill, and that makes her very angry.
But she's going ahead with her party.' John opened the
library door; the evening was over.

'I know you're invited,' she added; 'I'll see you
there . . .' Rachel walked across the dark hall. A night-
light was burning beside the porter's desk; shadows
crossed and recrossed the marble floor. The smell of cigar
smoke and perfume was heavy. John tugged back the
latch and pulled the door open. A London smell, of rain
and traffic and cold streets blew into the warm hall.
Rachel turned, and rested her hand on John's waist. 'I
really hope that I see you at Jodie's . . .' She took her
hand away just as John kissed her cheek. He could taste
sweet powder on his lips. Hill Street was deserted;
the air was milder and a fine mist was softening the
lights.

'I'll find a cab,' said Rachel, turning to leave. 'And
don't worry so much; get shallow – that's the summit of
wisdom.'

John wondered what Rachel meant as he watched her walking down the street, her head bowed and her pace quick and even.

Six

In the past, John had never paid much attention to the
potency of objects; now he lived through emblems of a
gaseous serenity, golden and talismanic, which he
snatched at, with increasing faith, from the furrow of his
routine. After a few days in Worthing, he returned to the
Chatham club, in time for Jodie's party. He brought with
him a few items, which, when arranged on the cracked
marble slab of his small dressing-table, could represent
his life and hopes. Jodie, he thought, would probably
have seen in this collection of odds and ends the making
of an apparatus for sympathetic magic – would have
suggested that their concentration, combined with his
own, might will a passage of events through their pattern
of symbols. Casually, at first, and then with clear inten-
tion, John built a shrine in his room at The Chatham.
He would be staying at the club until Christmas Eve; in
a new mood of fragile optimism, induced by the drugs
in his system, John was founding the image of a religion.
His deity was hope, and this most slender of content-
ments seemed sacred. He felt as though he was under-
going a conversion; he was – as Jodie had remarked about
his home in Worthing – the same but not the same. His

laziness had been replaced by a certain vitality; his curiosity had emerged from the shadow of fear.

His room was on the first floor, at the end of a dim corridor. Two long windows looked down into the street; plain furniture – a high bed on an elderly wooden frame, an old-fashioned telephone with a cord of pleated maroon threads – made the room ascetic and cell-like. A cheap Italian table, imported at the turn of the century, stood between the windows; its legs were made of iron, the marble which formed its top was pale, and, where chipped, faintly crystalline. A mirror hung above the table, its surface divided by a metallic smear. Having put his clothes away in the tall mahogany wardrobe, John looked at the oddments on his dressing-table. Their shapes and colours pleased him. There was a biography of Edie Sedgwick, bought because Rachel had mentioned her name; the photograph of Edie on its cover, printed in tangerine and turquoise, had reminded him, in turn, of Rachel. He propped the book against the wall, beneath the mirror; to its left he placed a thick white candle, perfumed with geranium. Two packets of French cigarettes, and a bottle of pain-killers, were set out neatly; his wedding ring, still brightly polished, was placed to the side of the shallow silver dish in which he had placed three crimson cones of incense. He added the souvenir calendar, out of date now, from the shrine of Saint Bernadette; in the central space he placed another book, *Listening To Prozac*, by Peter D. Kramer. The book was subtitled: 'A Psychiatrist Explores Antidepressant Drugs and the Remaking of the Self.' It was one of the few books which John had read from cover to cover, finding aspects of himself in each chapter. He left it open at his favourite passage; the book was American and printed on thick, ivory-coloured paper. He read, once more:

If I were to rewrite P——'s thought experiment today, I would have us imagine a woman – one who finds herself a castaway, always feeling like an outsider, somewhat sad, compulsive in ways that seem alien to her, quirky in ways that are only partly comfortable, over-sensitive to slights, limited in her capacity to enjoy the fruits of the island, a bit vague in her thought, listless, doubtful of her worth. She has struggled to ascertain the roots of her unease and per-haps has come a certain distance towards that goal, having made herself aware of difficult experiences in her childhood. But her mood and social circumstances remain unchanged, and so her search continues. Now let us imagine that as she walks along the beach she finds a bottle containing not a slip of paper but a number of green and off-white capsules filled with a white powder. Questing and desperate, she decides to take the capsules, one each day, and in time she feels bolder and less troubled, more at ease with herself, keener of thought, energized, more open to ordinary pleasure. Is there a message after all, a message in the capsule?

When he had first read this paragraph, John had read himself described; re-reading, he was reminded of Rachel, and thus the book was doubly qualified to be the secular Bible of his temporary shrine. The shrine pleased him, and he added to it daily: the blistered foil packet of his Prozac tablets; three relaxation tapes, a photograph of himself. At night, nearly asleep, he would smoke a cigarette and look at the portrait of Edie Sedgwick; his own self seemed to merge with that of the dead socialite, and the memory of Rachel. Rachel, he knew, was the scared flame which had turned his few ornaments into some kind of altar, beside which he never felt wholly alone.

Sarah Vick was relieved to see her cousin more at ease with himself. 'Whatever he's taking, it's working,' she said to Robert, who nodded his approval. It was Sunday. Sarah and Robert were having a late breakfast; the table was strewn with the day's newspapers and magazines. Later, they would go for a walk, and their afternoon would end, inevitably, at a repertory cinema or a busy street market. That was their Sunday routine. The day was cold and clear; the towers of the Barbican showed sharp profiles against the blue sky. The water gardens were covered with a thin sheet of ice; the frozen pools looked like slabs of onyx.

'Does John know that Anne's seeing someone?' asked Robert. Sarah tightened the cord on her bath-robe. 'I think he must do,' she said, 'but he didn't ask, so you can't tell.'

The previous night, John had dined with his cousin. He had seemed in better spirits, more voluble, and almost bashful about the earlier extremes of his depression. 'It's all very well,' Sarah continued, 'but the pills will only put a lid on things which he ought to be sorting out; they won't make him well. And what'll happen when he stops taking them?' Sarah did not trust chemical cures; she believed in the psychodynamics of therapy, psycho-synthesis, and Reichian bodywork. 'He ought to be seeing someone – a therapist.' She concluded, 'What about that woman who treated Sylvia for her food-abuse? She was really good . . .' The sun, inching around the tower, sent a shaft of white light across the kitchen table. Sarah squinted and shaded her eyes with the flat of her hand.

'Maybe he doesn't need all that – ' Robert spoke ter-sely; 'It could be a perfectly normal sense of loss; after all, they'd been married for a few years.' Sarah stood up, ruffling the back of her hair with her hand. 'Well . . . I'm going to have a bath,' she announced. She paused by the sofa to pick a fragment of water-biscuit off a cushion. John had become a responsibility, she felt; he had found a way into the bright Sunday morning to nag at her concern for her friends.

'Do you know,' she said, 'I asked him last night whether he was going to keep the house in Worthing . . . It's a lovely house . . .'

Robert looked up from his newspaper.

'And he said that he'd run out of money. Not a penny, he said – living on credit . . .'

Robert gave a low whistle. He had always resented John's private income, because he thought that it was wasted on a person who had no ambition and no ideals.

'I don't quite see how he could have spent all of it . . .' He raised his eyebrows, as though the news had proved some point in an unspoken argument. 'Well that won't help his situation – that's for sure . . .'

Sarah looked at her feet and wriggled her toes. 'He was telling me about a woman he's met – he seems really keen on her.'

'Oh.'

'Your father always said that other people's money and other people's relationships were impossible to understand.'

'True.' Robert poured himself a fresh cup of coffee and returned to his newspaper.

'Maybe he'll have to get a job . . .' called Sarah, as she made her way to the warm bathroom.

'True,' said Robert.

'And what are you?' a cultured, male voice was asking, 'an artist? Or an intellectual?'

Any reply was inaudible, drowned by the sudden swell of laughter which had risen like a wave, drawing its strength from a chorus of masculine guffaws, and then, at its loudest, folding over on itself to splash across the crowded room in a spray of giggled exclamations. In the centre of the laughter stood a giant of a man, in early middle age, whose curly hair was short and greying with a monk-like patch of baldness at its crown. His eyes bright with mischief – or venom – looked small and piercing in his round, childish face. This was Gasson. He stood head and shoulders above the small crowd around him, and he played to the group as a comedian would play an audience, neither conversing nor performing but conducting the spirit of the circle. He was dressed in a suit of charcoal-coloured wool; a cummerbund of burgundy satin caused his stiff white shirt-front to bulge above his waist. A bowtie of blue velvet drooped luxuriously beneath his shaven and powdered double chin. His laugh was a high-pitched crackle of amusement, teasing whoever had caused it; John noticed, with awed repulsion, that Gasson's large feet were shod in dainty patent pumps, also decked with a velvet bow. Here was a dandy in full sail, an effete galleon, riding the choppy waters of a mannered ocean with supreme confidence. In one hand, with his plump fingers curled about the gold-foiled neck, Gasson was holding a bottle of champagne; in the other he held his own tall glass, half-filled with sherbert coloured froth. He dispensed champagne to his little audience like a dog-trainer handing out treats; his height gave him an air of languid superiority, while the women around him drank in his every word, eagerly offering themselves up to be the butt of his quips. He was indulging a temporary court; his real interests lay elsewhere.

John had arrived at Jodie's party shortly after ten o'clock in the evening. He had reached Holland Park too early, and spent half an hour wandering the neighbouring roads. His imagination had been caught by the terraces and mansions, with their glass-canopied porches and mysterious gardens, still coated in the heavy frost which had not thawed all day. Some of the houses were closed up for winter, their wide windows were shuttered and barred, their shapes were black against the winter night. The frost made a stillness and an intimacy; the ornate houses were separated by secret paths, covered with curled and frozen leaves, which would lead to some deeper interior. The quiet suggested some strangeness which might be disturbed should one search for long enough; a mingling of time and place in which the loneliness of a dark conservatory, overhung by uncut, leafless branches, was suddenly brought close to an emptied shop window, or office lobby, flickering in the ghostly violet light of a poorly wired neon strip. John had reached Jodie's front door with some gratitude, thankful to have found his temporary place, away from the overwhelming indifference of the frozen city.

Jodie's tall house was set back from the road; a long garden, descending in shallow steps across overgrown terraces, was crossed by an uneven path. An ivy wreath was hanging in the porch. The door was opened by a girl whom John didn't recognise – a hired butler. Her broad smile made him feel not only welcome but wanted; she was dressed in black and had clear, pale skin. She seemed to stand for something which was both admirable and out of reach. She took John's coat. 'I hope I'm not too early?' he mumbled.

'Heavens, no. There are loads of people here already.' Another guest had arrived behind John, and her unwavering smile moved on: 'Hi! Can I take your coat?'

The hall, lit by tall white candles buried in stone vases filled with rice, resembled a sale of ecclesiastical fittings and ethnic artefacts. Heavy drapes of indigo velvet lent theatrical mystery. The marble tiles of the floor were shining; the air was heavy with incense. To John's right, at the end of the corridor, two more girls were standing by the door of the downstairs drawing-room; beyond them came the muscular volume of laughter and conversation. The girls were dressed in black and both were holding broad silver platters. On one stood tall glasses of champagne or herbal tonic, on the other was a bright tessellation of exotic canapes, garnished with wedges of lime and stems of basil. John took a glass of cinnamon-coloured tonic, sniffing at it cautiously as he entered the drawing-room. He felt conspicuous and solitary.

The room was divided by opened double-doors; many of the guests had retreated to its furthest end, drawn as though by some law of physics. They were older than John had expected. In the quieter half of the room, where two younger men, their faces set and serious, had been arguing, there was an elderly labrador, asleep on the rug in front of the fireplace. She belonged to one of the guests; 'Hello Penny,' said a dark-haired woman, kneeling to fondle the warm neck of the drowsy dog.

Much of the furniture had been rearranged; the room was brightly lit with lamps and candles; a double row of invitation cards, printed on stiff card, was propped against the gilded frame of the large mirror. Once again, John found Jodie's house oppressive; despite the finery and the exotica, there was an air of things which had been stored for too long, of strata of quasi-mystical detritus, of antiques uprooted from dark eras and savage circumstances. It was an atmosphere of the occult. John watched Gasson, fascinated by the cat-like manner in which this overgrown child seemed to toy with his admirers, charming them and mocking them while accumulating their trust. Gasson glanced at John for a second, raising his eyebrows as though acknowledging a co-conspirator in his waspishness, and hinting that they alone in the room were equals. John found this glance perversely flattering. He turned to search for Jodie or Rachel. New arrivals were constantly entering; socially, they were difficult to place. Dinner jackets and long dresses mingled with shabby suits, leather coats and old trousers; white hair and dyed hair was recoloured by the candlelight; ravaged, gaunt faces were attached to young bodies, while older guests appeared artificially youthful. 'What on earth do these people do?' John wondered. The accents were refined or exaggerated, broken here by French, German American and Russian. In the dark corridor which led to the kitchen, John saw the lace detonation of a match, throwing sudden shadows across the mural of framed prints which covered the wall. A man in a leather jacket was lighting his cigarette, standing alone and watching the crowd with hostile eyes. The expressionless stare of a Byzantine Madonna gazed fixedly over the shoulders of the crowd. John, with many ignored apologies, made his way through the throng towards the stairs. The mixture of scents – wine, perfume, incense and tobacco – was rich and heady. It was the scent of wealth, assurance and well-made things; it could never be bought or manufactured, it would only occur when the social chemistry was correct, and all the secret ingredients had been assembled by someone who had access to their individual strengths and characters. 'I wonder who these people are?' thought John. He was in awe of them. Later, he learned some of their names, and, from these names, drew an impression of a collective personality. The following people could be found among the crowd at Jodie's house that night:

George and Fiona O'Kelly, David Warren and Pam Spinner, Leon DuRoi and Stephanie Stone. Hugh Latimer, Cosi Latimer, John Ferrule and Mark Winston. Tim Higham, Pete Everley, Amanda Johns. Brian Anderson – the swimming champion – and Helen Chivers. Paris. The Hon. Sally Brakespeare. Tom and Naomi Fischel and their daughter, Emily. Lee Arnold, his dog, Penny, and Archie King. Beth Carter, from Los Angeles; Hannah Fitch, Rose Pew – daughter of the MP – Adrian Kiln, Helen Dobson and her partner Felice Troyat. Bruce and Hilary. Feist Chambers, Maurice and Pauline Minoche, Hans Ouler – who had caught a bullet in his shoulder while walking in north India, Jutta and Ben Warwick. Gasson Drewitt and Iris Vichy-Temple. A narrow moat of respect had formed around a famous pop singer. These were the heart and spine of the party, men and women at ease with their achievements. John did not find Rachel among them.

Upstairs, the broad landing was crowded; it seemed to serve as a subtle barrier between the younger generation and the older, the wealthy and the obscure. A girl with flame-coloured hair was leaning against the banisters talking to a drunk with gold teeth. A couple were kissing, their champagne glasses by their feet, on a chaise-longue upholstered in pink satin. John slipped by, hoping to see a face he recognised, and made his way into the first floor salon – Jodie's music room. It was hot and dark after the brightness of the landing.

This room, too, was crowded. Six church candles burned white on the mantlepiece. Embroidered cushions were scattered on the floor; rock music was playing from hidden speakers. The windows had steamed up – one had been cracked earlier on in the evening. The room was filled with young people whose faces looked drawn and satiated, angelic and childish, all at once; they were survivors of a decadence, living out a code of behaviour, the origins of which had been forgotten. A plump young man, his eyes lined with powder and sequins, was dressed in a tunic of mirrors. He was scooping cold soup from a bowl, his fleshy hands too big for his delicate china spoon. These guests, to John, looked like the punctuation marks in the footnotes of contemporary metropolitan culture: abandoned plans and wilted laurels seemed to jostle addiction and illness. Several people had looked at him when he entered the room; he felt as though they were predatory, yearning for pure blood. Their expressions were impudent, judgemental and censorious. A tall Spanish girl, spilling her wine down the front of her dress, looked in his eyes and laughed. Offended, John returned her stare, but she immediately turned her back on him and resumed her conversation. Her partner tittered, covering his mouth with ringed fingers. John felt uncomfortable; the company brought out his prejudices.

Finally, he caught sight of Jodie. She was receiving her guests at the furthest end of the room; she accepted compliments on her hospitality with a tired smile, and was kissed on both cheeks by a succession of well-wishers. Her neck and face were shockingly thin and pale; her long arms, when she stretched out her hands from the loose sleeves of her gown, were grey and frail. A cigarillo was dangling from the corner of her painted mouth; her thinning hair was pulled back into a bun, displaying long silver earrings. Around her neck she was wearing a wooden cross, and in her left hand, John noticed, she was holding a crystal which she constantly rolled between her fingers and her palm. Rachel was standing beside her, dressed in her usual uniform of black; her contact lenses were bright green and she smiled happily at John when she saw him crossing the room towards her. Jodie smiled, too, and stretched out her hand. John kissed Jodie's offered cheek, and felt a surge of happiness as Rachel leaned forward and squeezed his waist, affectionately. In an instant, his adoration of Rachel had increased because he had seen an answering light in her eyes. 'New lenses,' he said, pointing. Rachel nodded. 'How do you know all these people?' he asked, aware that Jodie was looking at him with some amusement. His voice sounded strange to him; blood was beating in his ears and he couldn't hear himself speak. 'Do you know many people here?' he asked Rachel.

'One or two, but not many. I've been waiting for you.' she added.

'There's Josh . . .' said Jodie, suddenly; 'Well, of all the cheek . . .'

'Josh wrote nasty things about one of our friends,' said Rachel, turning to John, 'and so we don't like Josh . . .'

The music grew louder. Rachel had positioned herself next to John. She seemed content just to stand beside him, watching the few people who were starting to dance. The dancers broke away from the edge of the room, finding confidence as they became absorbed in their gyrations. A woman in furs came up to Jodie, and Rachel turned her green eyes on John once more. 'I'm so glad you're here,' she said, and kissed him. The kiss was a sudden cold pressure on John's lips; it was gone before he was aware that it had happened, but it left his mouth tingling with a faint taste of peppermint. 'Do you dance?' she asked, resting her hand on his wrist.

'I'm afraid not . . .'

Rachel left John's side and spun into the edge of the dancers. She danced an abbreviated twist with the self-assurance of a professional; the music dated from Jodie's youth, sinewy American pop from the middle of the 1960s. Rachel was dancing to 'I'll Meet You at the Love In'. Jodie returned to John's side.

'You had a nice evening with Rachel I hear?'

'Yes. It was really good.' John watched Rachel, dancing alone among the flailing couples. His love was complete, and he knew that he had to declare it. Nothing, he thought, could alter his feelings; all other loves had been a rehearsal for the passion which he felt for Rachel.

John's good looks appealed to Gasson; his build, blue eyes and blond hair comprised a formula of beauty to which the older man was irresistibly drawn. He had noticed the solitary guest as soon as he entered the room, and had felt a sudden tightening in his chest, caused by desire, as his senses responded to the handsome stranger. When aroused, Gasson acted quickly; he disliked approaching a person whom he did not know – he found it vulgar – but he was expert in manipulating introductions. Years of bitterness had made Gasson jealous of other people's happiness. He had followed John upstairs, pausing for snippets of conversation, and had watched with sudden interest the intimacy between John and Rachel. He had seen the adoration in John's eyes when he looked at Rachel, and had read the reciprocal interest in her half-smile as she inclined her head to listen. Gasson could recognise, with a dramatist's eye, the stages of love and infatuation; all of his life he had longed for a love which never happened – he knew love by observation. He felt sad, for an instant, with the weight of hopelessness which he carried around with his loneliness. To combat this assault on his spirit he relied upon the character he had created for himself – mischievous, popular, malicious. Now that Jodie had moved on to other guests, and John was standing alone once more, smoking a cigarette, Gasson made his way across the dark room in several stages. His enormous figure and his imperious charm made him socially fearless. He wanted to corner

John — to explore an unknown country which might be conquered and added to his kingdom. He took whispered advice from Jodie, who laughed out loud at his question. John looked over and saw their faces turned towards him.

'We were just talking about you . . .' said Gasson. His voice was a sly drawl, laced with ambiguous amiability, but his words made John feel important, as though he had finally been offered the passport to Jodie's extraordinary society.

'Oh, really?'

'We were wondering whether you're always so hand-some, or whether it's just the light . . .'

Jodie beamed at John, as though pleased on his behalf for this compliment.

John felt compromised. 'I was just thinking the same thing about Rachel,' he said.

'Oh — Rachel. Do you know her?' Gasson moved closer to John, confronting him directly. John was aware of the warm, scented bulk beside him; he had to look up to answer.

'Vaguely; I'm a friend of Jodie's.' He offered Gasson his hand. 'I'm John.'

Gasson took the hand and murmured his own name as though it was of no interest to him. 'I should hope that you are a friend of Jodie's; otherwise what are you doing here?' He gave a snort, and squeezed John's elbow. His tone was suddenly donnish and patronising. John felt as though his new status had just been withdrawn; he tried to reassert himself, but could think of nothing to say. Gasson decided to play on John's feelings for Rachel.

'She is lovely, isn't she?' he said, speaking to John as an equal once more. John, who wanted to like Gasson, because he found him impressive, felt a surge of trust. Generous with happiness, he turned to Gasson as a friend.

'I don't know what it is, exactly,' he confided, 'but I think I'm in love with her.'

Gasson raised his eyebrows. 'But it is extraordinary, though, isn't it?' he said, 'Don't you think so?'

John nodded, confused. 'Yes . . .' He wasn't sure what Gasson was talking about.

'I mean,' Gasson continued, 'She must be so brave – to say nothing of strong.'

'I'm sorry?'

'Rachel . . .' Gasson felt a luxurious sense of power. John nodded, suddenly certain that Gasson was acknowledging Rachel's loyalty to Jodie. No one at the party had mentioned Jodie's illness. John became grave, lowering his voice.

'I just hope that she'll get better; that's all one can do.'

'Oh, I don't think that it's a question of a cure;' drawled Gasson, 'It's her own business, after all . . .'

John and Gasson, as the floor became more crowded, had moved into the narrow bay of one of the windows. Gasson was fascinated by John's understanding of the conversation. He sipped his champagne, waiting.

'The business must be the last of her concerns,' said John, earnestly; 'It's been such a strange year, though – so many people ill and depressed.'

'And Rachel, the picture of health and youthfulness . . .'

John nodded.

'Of course,' Gasson continued, his voice syrupy and his breath sweet with fine wine, 'there was a time when such a thing was unthinkable, to say nothing of dangerous. Two friends of mine in New York – do you know Bobby and Fred by the way?'

'No.'

'Well, several of their friends went through with it, in the Sixties, and got cancer from silicon poisoning; "She died of a silicon heart", as the song goes . . .'

'Where exactly is Jodie's cancer?' asked John.

Gasson suddenly clicked his tongue, his expression changing. 'Oh, you fool!' he snapped, suddenly, 'I'm not talking about Jodie! I'm talking about Rachel and her back street hormone treatment.'

John could not untangle the threads of the conversation. 'Rachel's ill?' he asked, aghast.

Gasson fixed John with a piercing stare. 'Rachel,' he said, slowly, 'is a man. At least, she's still got a dick – and that's what counts, isn't it?'

At Worthing, the sky was the colour of bruises and bone. A light lay across the horizon, a thin streak of gold. The winter sea sucked greedily at the beach, breaking heavily over the blackened groynes. The wind blew sleet and spray. On calmer days, at low tide, John watched fishermen digging for bait at the distant water's edge. He wondered how they could stand the cold. The town had never seemed so dull or so empty, despite the frail Christmas lights and the daily throng of shoppers. From morning till dusk the streets were lined with wet cars; in the evening, patches of fairy light gleamed between the shadows on the damp promenade. John, confused and light-headed, was trying to recreate his routine, searching for the therapeutic rut which had been born in the warmth of early summer.

Worthing had been reduced by Gasson's few words; to John, his small home town was both a crucible of painful memories and a place which had become unreal. But neither the pain nor the unreality seemed natural: glazed with Prozac, John's senses answered each mental challenge with a plastic heroism. He revisited cafés and corners where he had been happy with Anne; he felt as though he had betrayed his past, and, while vivid scenes ran like fragments of 8mm film through his mind, he no longer felt that he owned his memories. The lines of the white buildings were Anne, as much as the cushions on the sofa and the shadows in the corners of the bedroom ceiling. He never heard from her; but then his rudderless drift had been checked by Rachel, only to recommence, across far wider water, in the wake of the knowledge that his love for his wife had been replaced by love for a man. But because of Prozac, John thought, he was experiencing his emotional concussion at one remove; he felt impatient with despair – his faith in hope was intact. He could talk himself, without effort, into the belief that all would be well, somehow.

Only sometimes, when he was least prepared, did a sense of total sickness rise up within him; a reminder that, by way of drugs and illness, he had grown older as a different person. Glimpses of the enormity of this transition would drive him, momentarily, towards infantile comforts. 'I'll find Anne,' he would say to himself, or 'I'll call Rachel – get shallow . . .' And then, as his nervousness subsided before it could fuel itself, he would return to the pleasantly lit domain of his rut, where, because of the effect of Fluoxetine INN on the serotonin levels in his brain, hope remained robust and his sense of beauty endured. To perceive the reality of his situation had become impossible.

At first, John had thought that Gasson was drunk – or joking. He had looked at the wide, flushed, smooth-skinned face beside him and been ready to laugh. He had smiled at the incredible pronouncement, only to know, within seconds, that Gasson was telling the truth. Beyond Gasson's broad, grey-suited shoulder, he could see Jodie talking to a tall man; he had said, 'Oh, really?' and turned to watch Rachel, who was still dancing. The music had changed to heavy rock, levelling the elegant salon like a juggernaut. Still, it was as though nothing had changed, even as everything had changed. Rachel was still as beautiful, to John, her movements as exciting – and she was a man, with artificially induced breasts and hips. But John's bursting hopes had not turned into their reverse image; the consequences of Gasson's words were too complex and too sudden for him to reframe his emotions. He had longed to talk to Rachel, to question her and challenge her – but he had left, collecting his coat from the smiling young woman who seemed as unreal as the rest of the evening.

Taking a taxi, through Bayswater and down Park Lane,

John had looked at the delicate silver lights which were strung like diamond necklaces through the branches of the leafless trees. The cold had been intense; Rachel had become a blind spot in his mind. The following day he had returned to Worthing. He felt calm and lucid, most of the time. There had been messages and mail; Tony and Sarah both wanted to know that he was all right, and to wish him merry Christmas; he had more or less run out of money. There was a Christmas card, bland and opaque, from Anne. Finally, on Boxing Day, John had telephoned Jodie Kleist.

He rang her in the late morning; a woman whose voice he did not recognise had told him that Jodie was resting. Cautious, at first, the stranger had then been eager to talk, unburdening herself, it seemed, of the strain of silence. Her tone was nervous and elderly: she was eager to confide her fears in someone.

It's happening so quickly,' she said, 'I mean, it's so sudden, I don't know what to do . . .'

'I'm so sorry,' said John, uselessly.

'She's losing her hair,' the woman continued, 'because of the treatment, and sometimes she's so sick, and then she's so angry . . . It's heartbreaking to see her suffering so much . . .'

The nearness of death touched John too lightly. 'I saw her at her party,' he said, 'and she seemed much – '

'Oh, it's been terrible since then. I don't know how she stood it, really, I don't . . .'

'How do you know Jodie?' John asked.

'I'm her mother.'

In the afternoon, Jodie had telephoned John. He was surprised to hear from her, more surprised by the lightness of her tone. 'I gather you spoke to mum,' she said, laughing.

'Yes. She was nice. Jodie – '

'Hold on . . .'

There was a pause. 'Yes?' said Jodie.

'Is there anything I can do? I know you'll get better . . .'

'I won't; so there's no point hoping.'

It occurred to John that he had stupidly broken a rule of propriety; perhaps even Jodie's closest friends were no longer calling her whenever they felt like it. Perhaps, he thought, he had blundered towards the deathbed, blind to the tightening hold of the cancer.

'Rachel wants to take me away, somewhere warm,' said Jodie, as though she was speaking of a holiday.

'That's such a good idea; I really think you should go – if you can.'

'It won't matter soon. It's a case of "have drugs, will travel" . . .'

John listened to Jodie, amazed at her composure; he wondered whether all of the exotic and arcane books and ornaments which she kept in her tall house, had come to life in her hours of need to give her the strength to face the unimaginable. Perhaps, he thought, drugs and magic had united – the older medicine and the new. He remembered an earlier comment of Jodie's: 'Nobody takes illegal drugs anymore – the legal ones are much better . . .'

'Speaking of Rachel,' Jodie said, 'she wants to know why you haven't called her.'

'I want to call her. Gasson told me the truth, you know – about Rachel.'

'I've never seen anyone as lovely as Rachel,' said Jodie. 'He's a man . . .'

'He was a man; he's a beautiful person. And I thought that you were falling in love with him?'

John was silent. Jodie's cordless telephone transmitted a clipped surge of white noise as she rearranged her pillows, propping herself up on her thin elbows. 'Don't you think you're being rather unfair?' she said, 'Rachel really cares for you . . . Or does it make you feel better if I call him her?'

'I just don't know,' said John, 'How can I know?'

'I'm dying' said Jodie, 'and love seems very precious; my body might be a boat to cast aside when I reach the other shore, but my body would love to be loved . . .'

With no warning, John's memories of Rachel came pressing back into his mind: he saw her coloured eyes and her reticent expression; her air of strength, gentleness and self-defence. 'Thank you, Jodie,' he said, 'I think that Rachel should take you away – whatever.'

'She will. She cares, you see.'

Two days later, John received a white business envelope. In it, there was a polaroid photograph of Rachel. She was topless – or he was topless, so John reminded himself – save for a richly-textured bra of claret coloured satin. Her hands were behind her back; she was photographed from the waist up. With a rush of familiarity,

John studied the amateur portrait: the messy hair, the powdery eye make-up, the warm, golden tone of her skin. There was no message with the picture, and no note; John placed the polaroid portrait on his mantelpiece, next to the postcard calendar of Saint Bernadette of Lourdes. As the days passed, John began to have faith in a love which he had once believed impossible.

Seven

London, for an afternoon, was touched by a few hours of freakish spring sunshine. The weather belied the middle of February; John's spirits rose as he walked to Tony Wollen's office in Harley Street. Honey-coloured light showed dusty and golden on the window of a hairdresser's salon; there seemed to be a violet mist hanging over the end of the long, straight street. The terraces of tall mansions, each with their polished brass name-plates and imposing front porch, exuded the expensive simplicity of private medicine. Tony had been reluctant to see John as a client.

'Your own person should really deal with this,' he said.

'My own person simply renews my prescriptions; anyway, it's just some advice that I need . . .'

Tony looked odd in his small office, which was less grand than John had imagined. Besuited and faintly embarrassed, he faced his friend from behind a leather-topped desk. John took a seat in the sturdy leather armchair, thinking of the tales which the walls had absorbed of bulimia, abuse and bad luck.

'Strictly speaking,' said Tony, 'I'm not seeing you; I can't really offer you a referral, if you want one, and it isn't my job to hand out pills . . .' He peered in his desk drawer and pulled out a pad of plain paper. 'To be honest, I can only listen. Which I'd do anyway. So?' He tapped his blotter with the end of his pen. His curiosity was roused, but he was expecting to be bored.

It took John just twenty minutes to tell his friend about Rachel, her mixed gender, and the sense which he now had, just behind his eyes, of a cold knot of numbness, which he could feel as surely as if he'd rubbed ice against his forehead. His account was factual and impersonal; he had never discussed sexuality with Tony; they had always approved, amicably, of one another's women. Even John's broken marriage, to Tony, had seemed to slip without effort into the usual crises of maturity; it was a great shame, but it was not – as Jodie might have said – the end of the world. But now the young doctor was listening to his friend with concealed amazement, jotting down notes out of habit. John, meanwhile, felt as though the mild afternoon was promising him the path to recovery: Rachel had become more than a person to him; she was a state of mind, an inspiration to a new way of life, an emblem of recovery. When he had finished, John lit a cigarette. Tony was scribbling something, and asked without looking up, 'Are you still taking Prozac?'

'Yes.'

'And how long have you been on them?'

'About eight or nine months . . .'

'Any worrying side-effects?

'Only at first; at first, I felt like throwing myself under a bus.'

'But you didn't.'

'I still have this sense of entombment, though; these junk thoughts . . .' Looking at Tony, he felt as though they didn't know one another, that their meeting, under the thick glass of professionalism, had made them strangers.

'The junk is free-floating anxiety,' said Tony, 'It's latching on to your weakest points – your worst fears. But you're not still having actual panic attacks?'

'No; I just have extremely vivid dreams – not nightmares as such, but dreams which are too real and full of unease, and with a very definite sense of place . . .' John felt weary with the sound of his words; he was tired of trying to explain the sensations he experienced. Rachel had said that she knew what he meant, and that had made a fetish of his worries. 'Panic tries to sneak up sometimes,' he said.

'Like the last temptation.'

'I'm not with you?'

'When Saint Anthony thought that he'd resisted all of the devil's tempting, when he was at his weakest, a final temptation turned up and took him by surprise. The element of shock and fear in panic is what perpetuates the panic, making a self-feeding loop of anxiety. But the Prozac should put a stop to all of that – really, it will. Believe me . . .'

'What about Rachel? I haven't told anyone the full story; Jodie's guessed, but Jodie's ill . . .'

Tony shook his head. 'I heard, It's awful . . .'

'And it's almost our generation; I can't believe we're

not young anymore.' For a moment the two friends came close once more; Tony sighed and put down his pen. 'Have I shocked you?' asked John.

'I'd be lying if I said that you hadn't, but . . .' Tony shrugged. 'I don't think that there's a problem in psychiatric terms; we could say that you're being treated for clinical depression, but it's mild. Other than that, you think that you've fallen in love. So where's the problem?'

'The woman in question is a transsexual . . . I don't know how to respond, but I want to – which is against my nature, as I know it . . .'

'If you want to talk about varieties of love, we can do that over a drink. Or bring her round for dinner. You'd both be very welcome . . .'

John was touched by this; he was fooled by his friend's calm manner. Tony didn't think that John was ill, but he thought that he was making a terrible mistake, and hoped the infatuation would pass. He had decided that it would not be breaking professional etiquette to discuss the meeting with Rosemary. She, he knew, would be fascinated.

'Rachel said that she knew what it was like to feel entombed; that made me feel better . . .' said John.

'Most transsexuals feel themselves to be trapped in a body of the wrong gender. The desperation can lead to self-castration and all sorts . . . Actually, there was a Hungarian doctor, cited by a man called Stoller, who kept a kind of account about his growing up to be a transsexual. He was a very beautiful child who adored his mother and loved feminine clothes; as a teenager he tried to kill himself, twice. And then he enlisted in the Army – where he was decorated for bravery under fire . . .' John listened, fascinated. 'He married, and had quite a few children – but sex for him was like lesbian sex; he didn't actually think of himself as being homosexual . . .'

'What happened to him?'

'Well, this being the 1930s, and the doctor being a man of great moral principle, he simply suffered in silence. His only outlet was to wear a blouse beneath his shirt or a hidden bracelet; the rest of his daily life was a painful lie. And the saddest thing of all was that he concluded his memoirs with the words, "God so wishes . . ." It's all in a book somewhere . . .'

'I'd love to read it; I'd like to find out more.'

'But if you don't mind me asking, how do you know that Rachel cares for you?'

'I just know; you know, like when you're young and you finally meet someone you think is really beautiful, and you just know that they're attracted to you, too. It's like being a teenager . . .'

'God help you!' said Tony.

'Thank you, anyway,' said John, rising. 'I hope that I haven't embarrassed you or anything . . .'

They shook hands. 'Stay well,' said Tony, 'and stay in touch . . . That'll be one hundred and twenty guineas,' he added, smiling.

John remained in London. The sunny weather continued;

green shoots of daffodils and bluebells had grown up beneath the trees in Hyde Park.

'A sudden frost might kill them all,' said Rosemary, walking with Tony towards the pale cliff of hotels which lined Park Lane, and the dank subway which led to Mount Street. John did not answer. He was deep in thought.

'I don't know why I've been telling you all this,' he said, 'I've told Tony, I suppose . . .'

Rosemary turned up the collar of her coat. 'Confession's like adultery,' she said, 'It gets easier with practice – to say nothing of addictive.'

'I've just got this feeling that something new is going to happen; I wake up in the night sometimes, and it's like I can't wait for morning – which is odd, for me . . .' Rosemary seemed to be easy company; away from Tony, she performed less and listened more.

'It's all a long way from Anne,' She turned her pale face towards John; 'I saw Anne, you know, the other day . . .'

'How is she? I never hear from her.'

'She's married to her job, if you know what I mean.' John and Rosemary went down into the cold subway; ahead of them, at its darkest point, a man was sitting on a piece of cardboard, his knees drawn up to his chin, begging for change. Rosemary fumbled in her bag for a coin. 'Actually,' she continued, 'It's more like she's having an affair with her job. She takes it incredibly seriously – like you would a new partner – and she seems to more or less live in the office. It's like . . .' Rosemary handed the coin to the beggar, who accepted it with a weary nod. 'It's like she's really changed . . .'

'Or maybe she's just like she was before she met me. Did she ask about me?'

'She did, actually. She asked how you were, and whether you were seeing anyone . . .'

'What did you say?'

'Nothing. I didn't know what to say. Oh, and she asked about the house, too.'

'We'll have to sell it.' said John, 'If not next month, then some time soon . . .'

'Is that bad? I had no idea. Wow.'

'Just is,' said John.

They crossed the street and headed north; whiteish sunshine bleached the pavement. On the corner of Grosvenor Square, a sudden wind cut across them, reminding the couple that it was still only February. Rosemary turned her back to the cold gusts, and huddled in her coat. 'Jesus! Where shall we go for tea?'

'Anywhere quiet and cheap. Not The Marriott.'

The blue sky had turned ragged with cloud. They quickened their pace towards Oxford Street. John felt as though Rachel was watching his every move. In the busier streets, the thousands of people who made up the crowds seemed locked in their own small worlds.

'So what are you going to do? About the house?'

'Half of it belongs to Anne,' said John, 'because she pays half of the mortgage.'

'Still?'

'She never stopped; and I never spoke to her. But now I can't afford it any more.'

'I thought that you were rich.' Rosemary spoke with an American openness about money and sex.

'But I'm also a lazy slob . . . in case you hadn't noticed.'

'We always thought that living in Worthing was cheap'; said Rosemary, ' – Like Paris during the Depression.'

'Anne used to say,' said John, smiling, 'that there was a lot of money in Worthing. The widows of middle-management, bent accountants, people with a bit stored up for a rainy day . . .'

'That's why the place is so pervy. It drips perviness . . .'

'I like Worthing. It's kind of empty.'

In Duke Street, John and Rosemary sat in the window of a small café; facing them, across the street, was the low, dark entrance to an underground car park. There was a lengthy menu printed on white card behind the refrigerated display of the counter. The remnants of the day's ham, cheese and coleslaw gleamed wetly on plastic trays. 'They always have the same sandwich fillings,' said Rosemary, 'wherever you go. But that's okay.' She peered over her glasses.

'I don't want anything,' said John, 'Just a decaff.'

'Have you got any pain-killers? I have neuralgia because of the cold wind . . .'

'Solpadol or Relcofen. They're both quite good.' John took out a white sachet and a small brown bottle.

'What's Relcofen?'

'It's like Neurofen only it contains more ibuprofen. It's great. I heard about it from a person who had a bad abcess. You just take one.' He shook a bright pink pill onto Rosemary's palm. They were served their cups of pale, bitter coffee by a silent Italian woman. It was just after four o'clock in the afternoon. Rosemary rested her chin on her hand and watched the passing pedestrians: office girls with bags of shopping and rolled umbrellas, men in creased suits, boys in padded jackets.

'We're witnessing the death-grip of democratic consumerism,' she remarked, idly. 'Just beyond this city there's nothing but open country, corporate retail parks and heritage experiences. We're raising a generation of psychotics.'

John laughed at his friend's calm tone. 'Do you really think so?'

'Sure. There's nothing left now but shops and violent crime. Ask anyone.'

John nodded, watching the rush-hour crowds. They represented the life that Anne had yearned for, but he couldn't resent their presence, which was somehow comforting. He longed to see Rachel; but there were urgent matters calling for his attention: the sale of the house, his dwindling income. He had to speak with his wife . . . Why? he thought, 'Oh – to discuss the divorce . . .' he remembered. He noticed, not for the first time, that his emotions were no longer immediate; they came to him diluted, or insulated in some artificial brightness. Once, he had been overcome by the thought that his life was nothing when placed against the infinity of time or space;

he had induced a mild agoraphobia – there had been an endless succession of phobia, real or imagined. He looked across at Rosemary, who was watching the street without blinking. 'Do you know,' she said, 'someone has just spent thousands and thousands of dollars to find out that the colour which represents the early 1990s, socio-psychologically, is blue . . .'

'Oh, really?' said John.

Rachel hated anything old. She was glad that she could live in a brand-new apartment; she said that she couldn't stand the thought of being in a place which had absorbed other people's memories and other people's problems. Her borrowed apartment was on the sixth floor of a block which had been left unfinished; the first three floors were empty offices – vast, open-plan spaces with exposed wiring ducts between squares of temporary flooring which smelt of yeast. A time-switch and a thermostat were set to control the light and temperature, automatically, through day and night. Beyond the lines of tinted windows, silenced by sound-proofing, London carried on. A small lift took Rachel and her neighbour, another photographer, to their residential corridor. There were always sheets of glass, struts of aluminium and boxes of electronic components lying around in the corridors. The lift was reached through an electronically locked lobby, where unopened mail was stacked beside the door by a part time security guard. Rachel's neighbour was a Canadian, called Ron, but they seldom saw one another from one month to the next. Ron was short and plump; he

dressed in pale coloured clothes and walked with an enigmatic smile playing about the corners of his wide mouth.
Rachel knew that she was lucky to live in the apartment;
she was often worried that Jodie's generous friend could
take it away from her as easily as he had given her
the keys. 'Don't worry,' Jodie had said, laughing, 'He's
probably forgotten that he owns it. That's what rich
people do.'

Now that Jodie was dying, Rachel felt uneasy about
the tenancy; in the apartment, now, it sometimes felt as
though Jodie was dead already, and she was living in the
emptiness created by that death. Rachel had watched the
illness take hold of Jodie; it had not happened slowly,
but with tyrannical, merciless vigour. 'I'm all washed
out.' Jodie would say, as she lay down on her couch or
bed, her eyes sunken with weariness – dead eyes, it
seemed – and her shoulders frail and thin. She took mor-
phine to ease the pain; soon, Rachel had been told, Jodie
would have to take heroin. 'It seems funny,' Jodie had
said from her pillows, 'but when you're dying they let
you do all of the things that you're not allowed to do
when you're alive. Only you're too sick to enjoy it.'
Jodie lay on her bed for hours; on bad days she was filled
with bitterness and rage, picking arguments with anyone
who came near her. On other days she dozed and listened
to music: Mahler, Elvis Presley and Pink Floyd were her
favourites. Rachel would often stay to read to her.
Initially, when there had been at least the pretence of a
remission, Jodie had said that she wanted to hear Shake-
speare's Sonnets, The Koran, and Proust. A week later,

as Rachel was reading 'When forty winters . . .' Jodie stopped her, weeping. 'Just read me this,' she said, handing her a glossy magazine, 'I just want to hear normal stuff, about my life . . .' And so they read magazines.

John, for Rachel, had become entangled with Jodie's illness. Rachel had given up most of her friends a long time ago; when she started working for Jodie, as her assistant and her friend, she had closed down her mind to love. Jodie knew everything about her. But once, at a party, she had overheard someone say about her, 'She'll be a freak at thirty-five.' Since then, she had stopped going out. In the four white rooms near Liverpool Street station, with their view to the east where the streets of Whitechapel washed up against the monoliths of the City, Rachel had come to rest. She had very few possessions: a few clothes, a small TV, four books, a pocket camera and a bullet-shaped cassette player. She slept on a futon, kept her make-up in a supermarket trolley and used the crockery and chair which she had found in the flat. And with these comforts she was perfectly content; at night, she would microwave some vegetables, sprinkle them with walnut oil and sit on the floor to eat them. Then she would bathe, watch television or talk to Jodie on the telephone. Sometimes, before sleep, she would pray. She always woke early; conscientiously, she kept the apartment spotlessly clean. She liked to know that she could always leave at a moment's notice, and not leave anything of herself behind.

But Rachel kept a diary. It was large and leatherbound; its covers and pages smelt of face powder because it was hidden under her make-up. Each year, Rachel filled the pages of her diary with her quick, neat handwriting; and at the end of each year she destroyed it, feeding the torn-out pages into Jodie's shredder. She had written about John, since she had known him. In September of the previous year: 'Monday: Today was bad because I xxxxxx the night before. I've only got one sexual fantasy, the way that other people only have one car. It's always the same situation, and always the same words, the same phrases. Each time I xxxx I try to remember *exactly* the same words in my head. But now John is in my fantasy: he pushes me against hot glass as I xxxx him off. My forehead is damp against the soft hairs above his xxxx. But could I really be happy with someone like him? Today I was sick, again. My breasts are tender and I had a bad stomach ache in the shops with JK. She was going to buy me that belt but I wouldn't let her. She's kind enough already. But when I got home I found that she'd hidden the Clarins cream in my pocket. Rang to thank her but she was out. Where? Tonight, if John were to call, I'd ask him to come round. R.'

Rachel signed each of her diary entries; her sickness was a lingering side-effect from hormone treatment. She spoke in her diary as she would never speak to anyone. The entry for the day of Jodie's winter party was almost illegible; the writing deteriorated with each line: 'John was there. I felt like a teenager and danced for the first time in ages. But then he was told – by that fxx fxxx Gasson – before I could tell him. I was going to tell him; I really don't think it could change anything. The golden threads have been pulling and pulling and pulling. He and I both know that we can be happy. I pray for a task to prove that I want to be happy. What use is that?'

And finally, in her new diary, on a page dated 26th February, Rachel had written: 'John is coming here tomorrow. I want to give him everything.'

It was early evening. From where he was sitting, on the varnished floor of one of Rachel's empty rooms, John looked at the window, filled with dull gold light. The only sound, barely audible, was the low tone of the air-conditioning unit, gently shuddering behind a white slatted panel above the door. He felt perfectly calm; his thoughts, like a shallow river, gently flowing over pebbles and rocks and combing the long weeds with its warm current, were following a peaceful course. Everything seemed to be in its right place; for each fear there were corresponding hopes. Rachel was facing him, with her back to the wall, on the other side of the room. Beside John there was a white ashtray; mingled with his own cigarette ends there were three of Rachel's – white French filters which bore the light imprint of her bronze-coloured lipstick. Rachel was wearing heavily belted jeans over a black leotard; her pointed boots were scuffed. The white room was filled with her perfume, the scent of rain on a lush English field, cool and green. Her short hair was messy; in place of her coloured contact lenses she was wearing a pair of horn-rimmed reading glasses which rested halfway down her straight nose.

At times, during their conversation, John had been

bored. But Rachel's beauty overwhelmed him, and made the novelty of her every word and movement seem important. He tried to remind himself that he was in love with a transsexual; that Rachel's youthful body, with its broad shoulders, small breasts and slender waist was an artificially altered image of her own. It didn't matter. When he had felt her cool fingers stroke his cheek, for the first time, he had held the young man close to him and whispered, 'I love you, absolutely.' Now there seemed little to say; they were in total agreement about their feelings for one another. They had known that they would be lovers from the moment when John had entered the apartment.

Rachel, too, was a depressive: hopelessness had never seemed far away. She walked a thin line between perseverance and collapse, saying little, conducting her days with a quietness which belied her agitation – which she revealed only in her diary. Three years earlier, partially and painfully changing her sex – becoming Rachel – she had felt new confidence. In her mind, she had become a person whom she could now allow her body to represent; the complete loneliness of the transition had incubated her new personality. She had had the sensation of breathing more freely. The hormone treatment, drugs, hospitalisation and therapy had altered the channel of her nature; sometimes, her complex history felt packed, physically, too tightly within her. She would experience a suffocating sensation, as though one more memory or one more experience would fracture the fragile container of her body. This sensation, when it swept over her, would make her vomit. When John arrived, he saw the calmness in Rachel's eyes which had come from learning how to cope. He was in love with her strength and her promise of peace.

Following Rachel through the white, empty rooms, John had been struck by the space and the light; he had glimpsed an olive-coloured blanket, neatly folded beside a pink cushion, and a black leather jacket hanging over the metal frame of the only chair. But when she knelt down beside him to pour his tea, and looked directly into his eyes, he had heard the question, once more, which was being asked in Worthing, 'Can you love me?' Night fell, but the apartment remained unlit; the white rooms were dim and obscure, halved by shadows and cut with blocks of crepuscular orange light from the street. The air-conditioning and the heating maintained their soft, regulated sounds, like a muted nocturnal chorus. Rachel sat next to John, her arm around his shoulders. The world, it seemed, was before them, theirs to own; love, which had been their gaoler, had now opened the prison doors. 'That we're going to be together,' Rachel said, 'seems so right. I wasn't sure at first, but now I'm quite sure . . .'

At midnight, they went to collect John's two suitcases from the Chatham club.

'It's my last night there, anyway.' he said.

'I want you to stay with me . . .'

John watched Rachel pulling on her big leather jacket; it was old and creased, with a heavy belt around the waist and a thick diagonal zip.

'What a beautiful jacket . . .'

'It's a Perfecto – an antique. Jodie bought it for me in El Paso.'

'It's perfect on you.'

Rachel turned and smiled, 'Why, thank you' she said.

The street was cold and empty, the City deserted. It seemed as though the office blocks and shops had ceased to be real in the absence of their workers and customers. John pointed out the block where Sarah and Robert lived. They stopped beneath the high towers to light their cigarettes.

'I'm having supper there tomorrow,' said John, 'Would you like to come?'

Rachel shook her head. 'I don't really see anyone; it takes me months to want to see people. But come to me, afterwards.'

'I'm sick of this; really, really sick . . .' The words were out before Robert could stop them. His voice had risen and his tone was hard with anger. His statement had cut across the supper table, drowning the murmured conclusion to the conversation. Sarah turned sharply to look at him, fury and bewilderment mixed in her expression. 'Robert!'

John lit a cigarette, and offered one to April's new boyfriend, Steven. April sat back in her chair, like a pupil awaiting a scolding. Beverley and Richard, two of Sarah's oldest friends, looked aghast. Robert was red in the face and his hands were trembling. He was staring at his guests as though it was they who had shocked him. All eyes were on him. He flexed his fingers. John noticed that his jacket had slipped off the back of his chair.

'Wow,' said April, in an awed voice, 'that's hostile.'

'It certainly is,' said Sarah, grimly.

Richard's northern voice, friendly but concerned, cut in from the end of the table. 'Is there anything you want to talk about, perhaps?' The joke fell flat. Robert seemed exposed, more ridiculous than angry. Sarah got up from the table, her eyes wet with tears; her partner reached out wearily to touch her arm, but she took no notice.

'I'm sorry,' said Robert, 'but really, if you could just listen to yourselves!'

'That's not the point!' said Sarah, her voice rising. The guests at Robert's birthday supper stiffened once more. Steven rose quietly from the table and left the room, embarrassed.

Robert raised his head. His usual benign expression had vanished. John was reminded of a small boy who had suddenly thrown himself at his enemies, his arms flailing. 'I am sorry,' Robert repeated, 'but so far tonight . . .' he began to count the points on his fingers, 'we've had: antidepressants, psychotherapy, illness, phobia, cancer, stress-management, territorial hostility . . . hostility . . . What was it?' He gestured briskly towards April, who raised her eyebrows defensively, 'Oh yes, eating disorders, the difficulty of getting a job, hating the jobs we've got and the fact that London, which I happen to like, is a cross between a death camp and a sewer! Why does everything, every little thing, have to be a problem or a fear? It's so tedious – or really false, which is worse!

You all seem so happy with your problems and your crises . . .' He raised his voice once more, smacking the table with his fist. 'Go ahead! Bow down before the great god Depression! Swap drugs! Become career neurastheniacs! But leave me out of it; I don't want to know!'

For a few seconds there was silence, then a chorus of voices all broke out at once.

'Listen, all I was trying to say . . .' said April.

'You're choosing that response – ' said Beverley.

'What would you like to talk about?' said Richard.

'You're probably right,' said John.

Sarah, however, said nothing. She cleared the plates from the table and took them into the kitchen. She was embarrassed and upset. It seemed to her that Robert had betrayed the collaboration which had always existed between them. From the little kitchen she could hear the sound of animated voices, the noise of polite society trying to mask its raw feelings. She knew that the incident would pass – had passed, already – but when she thought of the wide bed which she shared with her partner she felt as though it would never be the same again. When she returned with the dessert, a discussion was in progress.

'But in this book,' Richard was saying, leaning forward to make his point, 'the guy is saying that most of his patients aren't actually sick – it's society that's sick and we've got to come to terms with it . . .'

'And all I'm saying is that not everyone shares that opinion,' said Robert, with an uneasy smile. 'I think that you're all too complicit with victim status, that you actively want a society in recovery, as though we only exist by virtue of our sickness. It does seem indulgent . . .'

'Maybe your problem,' said April, slyly, 'is that you don't want to see your problems . . .' Robert did not reply. He lit a small cigar.

'John told us that God knows how many million people are now taking Prozac; well, I don't mean this as a criticism of John, but I'm sick of bloody Prozac! It's just the new thing – the obvious successor to librium and valium and the rest, the mummy's little helpers that crippled a generation of working mothers . . .' He paused. 'I suppose that as an architect I'm trying to find ways of making people's environments, at least, a bit better than they were in 1962 or 1952. And sometimes I wonder why I bother . . .'

At this, Sarah rested her hand on Robert's arms and squeezed it, tenderly. Here was the idealist she loved – his temper was justified. Robert smiled at her. The little raft of their union was secure once more; their bed would carry them safely through the night, as usual.

'John's got a new girlfriend!' Sarah announced; 'Now that's good news!'

Eight

Anne Champney had thought of John, often; he was still her husband, after all, and their years together would not just slip away, as though they had never been. She knew that she had left John wretched; she had thought that her silence would heal his wound – but news of one another, like muffled voices from adjoining rooms, had reached the couple throughout their separation. Now, from her seat on the top deck of a London bus, looking out at the heavy March rain, Anne was close to the memory of her marriage. The bus, shuddering in a queue of cars, inched towards Blackfriars; she could hear the scraping of its windscreen wiper, the dragged arc of perished rubber over wet glass. The dusk cargo of weary passengers, heads bowed over their newspapers, or their eyes fixed, unblinking, on some point in their thoughts, was occasionally disturbed by the stooped entrance of a new traveller, grimacing and soaked, bringing with them the cold scent of rain. Mottled condensation, bejewelled with street-lit droplets, obscured the view of the river. The late afternoon had turned to night. Anne could see office blocks, bathed in sodium orange and swaddled in shadows, beyond the black span of a bridge; coming towards her, the twin diamonds of headlights, in endless succession, their white brilliance fractured. Gusts of rain swept over the bus as Anne gave way to nostalgia.

A chance encounter with Tony Wollen had opened Anne's mind to this reverie. He had spoken of the fall-back positions of nervous illness connecting John to this theme, and out of his words a strangeness had emerged – a mingling of fear and urgency which had shown itself in the reddening of his cheeks and a slight backwards tilt of his head. For a psychologist to be so clumsily open! thought Anne, fingering the small blue bottle of lavender oil which she had bought during her lunch hour. She had been walking down Wigmore Street when Tony saw her; he had stopped on the pavement and opened his arms wide in a gesture of welcome. But with their small-talk there had been the sudden tug of intimacy, tripping a switch too quickly that had opened an area of conversation which was too large for either of them to get their bearings. Tony, risking friendship, had not been able to hide the truth from Anne. His professional duty to John, to remain silent, had not been equal to the need – increased a thousand times when faced with the emptiness of Anne's expression, her bewilderment and innocence – to finally unburden himself of the secret. 'Do you know something about it?' Anne had said; her calm tone had not concealed the appeal in her voice. Tony had let out a deep sigh; he had stared at the pavement with swimming eyes. The tug was too strong for him; sensation battled with compassion. Lost, he had babbled, shocking John's wife into a silence which he could not penetrate.

The bus lurched, jolting the passengers forwards; there

was a shout in the street and the long angry tone of a car-horn. Another jolt and the bus moved on, veering slowly north. Tony's phrases, incredible to recollect, had fixed in Anne's mind. She didn't know what to think; the details seemed to be beyond thick glass, a membrane between the known and the unknowable. 'A man who was a woman, in love with John', 'The girl was a boy all along, and by that time . . .' She had not known how to react – stupid to assume she would – and Tony had realised the enormity of his news in a confusion of crossed-wires and tangled emotions. 'The strain of even being alive could become impossible . . .' Anne, in her fear, had hated Tony.

In Farringdon, loosed from grid-lock, the bus swayed with sudden speed. A low mist had fallen across that part of the sodden city. Anne, her thoughts unchecked, had remembered the mad man at Worthing: her neighbours had found him one night, wandering along the beach, half-naked and incoherent; his white shins were muddied with the freezing, silt-thick surf. They had taken him to the windowless shelter; his face was the face of a sad child as they waited, not talking, for the police, the ambulance and the grey hospital blanket. John was not one of those, she knew; his illness was an aberration – if he was ill at all. His new lover, he or she, was another stray; sorrowful, yes – Anne had no prejudice – but not good for John.

At Moorgate, Anne rose from her seat; clutching the rail she pressed the scarlet button with her thumb and a distant chime rang out. She would make it all all right, if she had to. But could she? The bus drew up to its stop and the cold rush of air fell away. Tall and neat, her long blue overcoat wrapped around her, Anne stepped down to the wet pavement. She was facing the towers of the Barbican, where John's cousin was waiting for her. Their adult lives, she had decided, must not be ruined; everyone made mistakes. If John was on drugs she would take him off them; if he was sick, she would make him well again.

The daffodils which Rachel had bought had just had time to open. Their double yellow flowers stood out against the white wall, suffused with green. It was midnight. In the next room, John was sleeping; he lay on his stomach in the centre of the white futon, the loose, ivory-coloured duvet pulled up to the small of his back. There was an ashtray beside him, filled with Rachel's cigarette ends and his own. The white room held no other furniture; the long window, with its deep, empty sill, was uncurtained. Sixteen candles were burning in the apartment; their yellow flames were straight and erect, barely wavering in the currents of conditioned air. The white rooms led straight into one another, with no doors between them.

Rachel had risen earlier; she had slept beside John since late afternoon. Wrapped in a white robe, she looked across at the warm, brown body of her handsome lover; his breathing was soft and regular, his eyelids still. It was nearly three years since Rachel had shared her bed. That afternoon, reaching to take a glass from the shelf, she had closed her eyes as John had pulled her towards him. He had slipped her leather jacket, heavy, cold and perfumed, off her shoulders, kissing the side of her neck and pressing the warm palm of his hand, gently, against her flat stomach. She had turned to look up at him, neither smiling nor frowning.

'You're so beautiful,' he had said.

'But I'm not a girl,' She had pushed his hand between her legs, watching his eyes, 'We're the same, see?'

The white rooms had been growing dim; shadows and edges were blurred lines of grey and blue. Outside, the silhouettes of the buildings were black against the pale sky. 'It's you,' John had said, 'It's just you that I want.' He had held her so tightly that she couldn't breathe; loosening his grip he had lowered his mouth to bite her shoulder with a kiss. He had felt the strength in Rachel's arms as her body responded to his; he had been fascinated by her sex, ravenous to possess her. He had held her down, looking at her slight smile; he had stroked her as she pulled his face down to her own.

When they had finally rolled apart, they were hot and exhausted. John had felt no anxiety. 'I love you' he had said, simply.

Rachel had lit a cigarette. Turning, she switched on her ioniser, watching its tiny scarlet light flash on. She handed John a bottle of water, having drunk from it herself. 'Your pill,' she had reminded him. She opened a small plastic wallet, and took out her vitamin pills. Bars of amber-coloured light lengthened and shortened across the small grey screen on Rachel's bullet-shaped cassette player; the room was filled with a soft sound: distortion, a drum beat, an electric viola and chanting. The tape sounded old, recorded on amateur equipment. The music was harsh, sweet, buried and mesmeric.

'Tell me,' she said, 'have you ever slept with a man before?'

'Never.'

'Not even in your fantasies?'

'No. Anyway . . .'

'What?'

'You're just you; it just is – that's all . . .'

John had been drowsy. 'It would all be fine,' he had said, 'if it could always be like this.'

'Like what?' Rachel asked.

'Just like this – perfectly happy . . .'

'It isn't much to ask,' Rachel had said, 'is it?'

The room grew dark as John fell asleep. Rachel had showered, greased her hair and put on her robe and glasses. She had called Jodie's mother, to ask for news of her friend.

'She had a shot,' said Mrs Kleist, 'and asked for you . . .' Rachel coloured.

'I didn't hear the phone; I could have been out.' Rachel bit her lip, and ran her fingers through her wet hair. 'Is she well enough to travel?' she asked.

'Not really – but she's set on going with you . . . The children are with their father, you know. Jodie doesn't want to see them. They hardly know anything . . . Where are you going, in France, at this time of year?' Jodie's mother sounded tired, her voice frail.

'Hasn't she told you?' said Rachel, 'We're going to Lourdes . . .'

'Is that what Jodie wants?'

'I think so, yes . . .'

Then, Rachel had watched John sleeping, her thoughts divided between her friend and her lover. An era was reaching its end; time was shedding its skin, leaving its transluscent image in the grass. It was unlikely that Jodie would live to see the spring; Rachel knew that. She had this idea that Jodie's soul must not be lost, and her instinct had turned into a fierce desire to take her friend to the southern shrine. Once that had been acknowledged, Jodie had said, some ritual would permit the new life; she and Rachel had discussed the notion, determined to see it through. Jodie, in illness, had matched her desire for superficiality with a return to the mysticism of her youth. Rachel closed her eyes, and longed for the new life. She was almost ashamed of the happiness which she enjoyed with John; it was new to her, and premature. Walking slowly around the apartment, she blew out the candles, one by one, and then she lay down beside John. The two men slept together peacefully, their fingers entwining at dawn, when they murmured one another's names.

'I'm never expected to cry,' said Anne, looking up through tear-filled eyes. 'I'm meant to be the stable one.' Huddled in her coat, which she would not take off, Anne had sat on the edge of Sarah's sofa with her briefcase beside her feet, finally giving way to the shock of Tony's pronouncements. There were raindrops in her hair, and she had brought with her the atmosphere of the working day. Sarah, watching her, had suddenly realised how tired she looked; Anne's neatness, close to, was like a thick varnish which was fracturing beneath hundreds of hair-fine cracks. New layers of varnish had been added, each coat more precise than the one before, but these could not disguise the decay underneath, the lack of restoration, and the tell-tale signs of exhaustion. Her strong face had hollowed beneath her cheekbones, her brown eyes were small and red beneath powder and mascara. Already, as though she was afraid of being overseen, she was holding a small mirror close to her face and dabbing her nose with powder. Her strength, now, resembled a heavy weight, painfully carried. 'I lost something, too;' she had said, 'nobody seems to understand that . . .'

Sarah, silenced, was reeling from the news that her cousin was in love with a transsexual; neither her liberal tolerance nor her compassion could reduce her amazement. 'I had no idea,' she kept repeating, 'I had no idea . . .'

'How do you think I feel!' Anne said; 'I just don't know what to do. I want to go to him, because it all seems so unbelievable, but at the same time I just don't want to get involved . . .'

'You ought to see him, I think . . . Really – '

'I blame Prozac,' said Robert, suddenly, 'I agree with Anne. I think that this whole thing about John has gone far enough . . .' Robert, soaked and tired, had arrived home in the midst of Anne's tears; he had been surprised to see her, but he could not feel any sympathy for the crisis. Increasingly, he felt, he was losing Sarah to the line of her troubled friends, whom she listened to patiently, and, he thought, to the exclusion of their own intimacy. There had been a time, not so long before, when he would have instantly entered into the spirit of the drama – the anaesthetist to Sarah's surgeon – taking his place on the edge of the scene as though the nourishing fruit of his love for Sarah depended on it. Now he resented that subordination to Sarah's surgery; he thought that she was becoming dependent on her friends' problems. Robert had problems of his own, with the air in his practice being less laced with the near-chemical scent of potential. He thought of his retirement; the prospect of a small house, dozing between vineyards and white country roads, seemed more inviting with each grey London morning. The time was approaching, he felt, for the coolness of tiled rooms behind sun-baked white shutters, and for fewer things to matter. That had been their goal. But would they have enough money? Sarah, it seemed, was content in her role as comforter; he was not.

Sarah was sipping her glass of red wine. The room was warm with yellow lamp-light and there was a smell of ripe fruit. Anne felt exposed and bitter.

'Even last summer,' she said, 'I remember walking through St James's park early one evening, and feeling just happy. There was nothing special going on – I just felt like I was myself again, after years of Worthing and not being myself – for John . . .' She sniffed, and sighed. 'I do still love him, I suppose. And there's the house . . .'

Sarah leaned forward. 'Shall I tell him to ring you?'

'Can't I ring him?'

'I don't know the number. He's not at The Chatham any more . . .'

'That dump!'

Anne looked helpless; she was still in shock. 'I'll have to see him, I suppose . . .'

'Who knows,' said Sarah, 'it might be the best thing you could do.'

'He could call me at the office. Not tomorrow, though; tomorrow's a bad day.'

When Anne had gone, Robert turned to Sarah with a smile which seemed triumphant.

'You know, I'd never have thought that Anne was the self-pitying type,' he said, calmly. Sarah did not reply.

Two weeks went by. Cold rain set in, thin and spiteful. It fell from the grey, monotonous sky as though it had always fallen and would never stop. In her quiet house, surrounded by incense, powders, books and shawls, Jodie Kleist had told her impassive children that she was going away for a little while, with Rachel. She wore a silk turban and a long white gown; her children could barely recognise her, and they seemed more resigned than sad. They had never seen much of their mother, whose moods were so unpredictable. The tall house was still; Jodie had asked for all the shutters to be folded back, so that she could watch the early spring rain. The evenings made her depressed, because they would soon be growing longer. For much of the time she slept, in a deep, drugged sleep. Her doctor visited every day.

'You should go to France,' he said, 'You can afford

whatever attention you might need, and, who knows . . .' He closed his bag and picked up his coat. He was young and Jewish, one of Jodie's social circle; he looked like a wealthy Italian businessman, with his severe silk ties and tailored suits.

'She was a remarkable woman,' he had said to one of his partners, already speaking of Jodie as though she was dead.

With Rachel, Jodie had spoken quite openly. 'I'm going to Lourdes,' she said, in a soft voice, 'because I want to, and because it might be warmer than here . . .'

'We both know why we're going.'

'To appeal to the blessed Saint Bernadette . . .' Jodie leaned back on her square white pillows.

'She helped me,' said Rachel, 'she might help you.'

'Oh, Rachel, how can I even hope for help?' Rachel held Jodie's hand, gently.

'Give me a cigarette,' said Jodie.

'You're not meant to . . .' Rachel lit a cigarette and handed it to her only friend. Jodie inhaled, weakly. 'That's gorgeous,' she said, 'if only it didn't hurt so much . . .' She rested her hand on the sheets; the cigarette slipped between her fingers and she looked at it with mild curiosity.

'Is it time for your shot?' asked Rachel.

'I've given up guessing. Half of the time I don't know when the drugs are working, anyway . . .'

Rachel nodded. She knew that Jodie was now permanently drugged; her mother had said so. 'We leave in two days,' she said, 'that's Friday . . .'

'Buy loads of magazines; all the good ones – any of them . . .'

'We're staying at the best hotel; I've brought you the brochure . . .'

Jodie smiled. 'Leave it on the table, thanks; I'll look at it later. What time is it?'

'Just after nine.'

'Can you stay tonight? Or are you leaving?'

'I can stay; I've brought my stuff.' Rachel walked across the large room and looked through the compact discs which were piled on a low carved table.

'Elvis Sings Gospel, Ravel or the Floyd?' she asked.

'Ravel. The piano pieces . . .' Jodie watched Rachel, kneeling in front of the record-player. Rachel was dressed in black, as usual; her contact lenses were cornflower blue. Jodie's bedroom was painted the colour of dried lavender, with silver woodwork and a pale blue carpet. The room, unexpectedly, was soft and feminine; there were old oval mirrors, their wooden frames crudely whitewashed; there was a sewing-basket, an iron wash-stand and a chaise-longue covered in bright silk cushions. Rachel had brought a bowl of white hyacinths; their strong, moist perfume filled the air. Most of all, Rachel was surprised by Jodie's attitude to her children. She knew that Jodie had never really wanted a family, and that her marriage to a shy, ambitious lawyer had been unhappy. But the children were seldom mentioned. 'It would have been better if they'd never known me,' Jodie had once said, while driving her fast car through Hyde Park, towards Kensington. A cheroot had been dangling from the corner of her mouth; a tiny log of white ash had fallen on her dress. She had brushed it away, and changed gear with a hard jerking back of her wrist.

'Tell me about John White,' said Jodie, reaching for her glass of grape juice.

'Is it serious?'

Rachel slumped down in her chair. 'I love him – I think . . .'

'And he?'

The transsexual raised her eyebrows and pressed her knees together. 'He says that he loves me, but . . .'

'Don't you believe him?'

Rachel made the gesture of a narrowing gap between the thumb and middle finger of her right hand. 'Almost . . . Yes; I do.'

'He's very handsome; you're extremely beautiful,' said Jodie.

'But he's never known anyone like me before; he's quite a simple man.' She paused. 'A bit lost, if you know what I mean . . .'

'Like Simon?'

'Oh, Simon knew that he was a lost soul. He was just putting off the day when he had to face it . . .'

'And Simon loved men.'

'But he pretended to love women.'

'And John? A married man?'

Rachel sighed, and then smiled. 'He loves me,' she said, 'me – person, not me, biological phenomenon.'

'Where is he now?'

'At Worthing. He has to talk to his wife.'

Jodie looked up but Rachel's expression was inscrutable. 'Aren't you worried?' she said.

'What will happen, will happen – I've learned that,' said Rachel, 'And he has to learn how to make decisions. I think he's been asleep for years.'

'Waiting for you . . .' said Jodie. She leaned back, exhausted. 'Burn some oil,' she said, 'and tell me about Lourdes.'

Rachel tried to describe the pilgrim's route towards the Pyrenees. She hadn't got far when she realised that Jodie was asleep.

When John arrived in Worthing, he walked with his bag from the station to his home through streets that were blue with the early spring evening. The walk was long, but he had slept in the warm, airless compartment on the train, and he felt refreshed and alert. The evening was mild; the trees, still bare, were shamed here and there by showers of white blossom. The fading light made the depths of old gardens, following the curve of the road, jump before his eyes. The breeze was sharp, with a salt edge; twin church spires, Anglican and safe, showed black against the pale blue sky. The evening star shone brightly beside the cold white crescent of the moon. He turned a corner. At the end of the wide road, receding through limitless shades of grey, rising into blue, were the sea and the sky. The wind picked up. The houses and hotels along the promenade, their contours so familiar, made him think that they had been waiting for the traveller to return. John felt their reproach; it seemed to him that he had been away for years. He recognised the landmarks of his morning walks: the blackboard outside a wine merchant's shop, a broken pane of glass in the roofed porch of a boarding house. This was his home town, but even as it welcomed him, not questioning his loyalty, he no longer felt at home. Approaching his own front door, which seemed to mark the barrier between his old life and the new, he wondered whether the snags of fear which were necessary to know emotion – the grit that made the pearl – had been smoothed away by anti-depressants; without that fear, the necessary fear, perhaps he was no longer capable of engaging with his conscience and his consciousness. But the old fear had been too much to stand, whatever it had been and wherever it had come from. Now, absorbed in Rachel, his chemical angel watched over him, turning anxiety to mild curiosity; nostalgia had brought him to Worthing. His wife would arrive the following day, determined to discuss their lives. John felt no excitement; he wished that Rachel was with him, to remind him of the first time when he saw her, blinking and ill at ease, on the edge of a shadow.

The following evening, when John sat facing his wife, he felt like a person being called to account for stock they had somehow lost. As he studied Anne's features, it was with the cold fascination of a lover re-reading an old love letter, the contents of which had been forgotten, but the discovery of which, years later, was a disappointment, belying the reality of the actual pages. Adrift, Anne looked different to him. Her hair was longer, and lightly waved, her wit and generosity, the twin charms which raised her from the crowd, appeared to have vanished in grimness. She was no longer wearing her wedding ring; her expression, so unlike the emptiness of his own, seemed to urge the mutual acknowledgement of some new set of rules . . . John, irritated, felt as though certain assumptions were being made, in silence, none of which he had agreed to accept. Lighting a cigarette, John felt distant from boundaries. Surprising himself, he was more curious than disturbed about the encounter which, for himself, he had run like film through his mind, cutting in sequences with lessening certainty, until the screen was finally, blissfully, blank.

Anne was angry. Her feelings for John had become confused, out of alignment with her intentions. When she had left Worthing, and left John, travelling on the sleepy Sunday train to London through a heat wave, she had thought that her mind was made up. On that warm evening, the capital had been warm and gold, cut with deep shadows beneath the blue sky, peaceful at the end of a hot, cloudless, day. The sea at Worthing would have been sparkling in the same brilliance; for John, falling into the chasm of fear and sadness, the trippers and the evening alike had seemed far away, and unbelievable. How could life go on, when his own appeared to be over? But London had welcomed Anne, and she had welcomed London; her jubilation had eclipsed that part of her imagination which might picture John in his misery, and drive her, with fatal sympathy, back to the small coastal town.

For those first months, she had missed her husband

but not her marriage; she had fought hard not to contact him, believing this to be best. She felt guilt, but she knew that love had betrayed her sense of purpose. She wanted to work and be busy. A flat, job and boyfriend had entered her life, like a new plastic spine created by a process of molecular multiplication, in which each acquisition was a new vertebra. Seeking evidence to support her new way of life, her sense of independence was sustained by the society of friends who shared her ambitions and her beliefs. She threw herself into her work; work was her new deity, the office her new church. She was repulsed, like any convert, by the infidelity of her past to this new creed.

'You've changed,' said John.

'You mean, I'm not how you want me to be. Is that it?'

'No; but . . .'

Anne's face was set and serious. 'What are you doing, John? What's going on? I think I have the right to know . . .'

John stretched, saying 'Ah . . .'; Anne mistook his tone for playful self-satisfaction. Her anger increased. She felt dowdy and bewildered.

'What are these pills you're taking?' she asked, briskly.

'They're antidepressants; I . . .'

'You don't need antidepressants!' said Anne, with a contemptuous snort.

'Well; after you left, I started getting . . .'

'I know all that; Tony told me.' Her voice altered. 'This is so horrible.' John nodded.

'I was thinking about our lions,' said Anne, 'That whole world we had . . .'

'I know; I remember it, too . . .'

'The thing about lions was that they stuck together – getting on. You stopped being a lion years ago . . . And that's what I lost . . . It broke my heart, John; and now it seems like a lifetime ago . . .' Her eyes shone. 'Nobody wants to admit that,' she said, her voice trembling, 'I lost something, everything, before you lost me. I didn't want all of this.'

John was silent. He was shocked that he could feel no sympathy for Anne.

'There's the house,' he said, gently.

'Is that it! Is that all?'

'What else could there be? We've both changed, and it's probably all my fault.'

'You sound quite happy with the situation . . .'

'I don't think that I can change back, now. There was a time – '

'Before Rachel?' Anne produced the name with a thin note of triumph. John sighed. 'Yes. Before Rachel.' He looked up. 'But you've had boyfriends too . . .'

'And I'm glad!'

'So, Rachel . . .' John barely pronounced the name; he was unwilling to connect his love to the conversation.

'I couldn't give a shit what sex he is . . .' snapped Anne.

John smiled, despite himself.

'Go on;' said Anne, 'You're so fucking proud of it . . .

You've finally done something that people can talk about . . .'

John shook his head. 'Don't be ridiculous. Anyway . . . I don't know what I'll do . . .'

'You're going to have to do something, aren't you? Well?'

'Yes . . .'

Anne's shoulders dropped, and she was silent. She felt exhausted. 'This is stupid,' she said, flatly. 'I thought that I wanted to save you, or something; but you don't want to be saved, and . . .'

'Yes?'

'I don't really want to be a saviour . . .'

The couple looked at one another. John remembered a phrase, but couldn't think where he had heard it, 'I feel better than well . . .' He couldn't understand why people had problems. 'How's your job?' he asked, finally.

'Good. I'm enjoying it. I'm going to Germany next month, Italy after that . . .'

'Oh, really? You'll enjoy that.' John wanted to say that Rachel had taken Jodie to Lourdes.

'Have you heard anything about Jodie?' asked Anne, suddenly.

'No.'

Anne stood up, carrying her coffee cup to the kitchen. 'I hope that we're still friends,' said John.

'I hope so, too.'

John looked for the magic in Anne which he had never used to question. She seemed reduced; the romance of the re-read letter had been given away by a familiar script and phrases which were too well-known. But in the back of John's mind, he was sure that it was not Anne who had failed to fill the place set aside for her in his heart; rather, he had used her up. His new mind, which made panic and tears equally impossible, was content to contemplate the surface and the shallows – skimming there for food and light; the depths were as difficult to fathom as the logic of a dream. The house would be sold – the money divided; Rachel would return to him and be different to Anne, a new promise of love.

That night husband and wife slept in separate rooms. Tired, John waited for a sleep that would not come. Finally, towards dawn, his eyes grew heavy and his thoughts began to wander; he thought of Anne – did her problems exist when she was asleep? He thought of the empty streets near Liverpool Street, at night – how they needed their workforce to exist. He thought of Rachel. Lastly, on the brink of sleep, he pictured an African plain, wide and scorched; he followed two furrows of broken white grass, leading to hot pale rocks. There, a lion and lionness lay side by side – so familiar to him. They had limped to this dry resting-place, their bony shoulders working tired flanks and their heavy hands drooping with fatigue. The sun had scorched their backs; but now they were dead, stretched out in the still heat, with flies crawling over their lifeless eyes.

The next evening, when John let himself into Rachel's silent apartment, the first thing he noticed was the sweet, smoky scent of jasmine. The white rooms were filled with the heavy perfume, a rich, faintly ecclesiastical scent, at once comforting and mysterious. At first, in the fading light, John did not see the solemn arrangement of statue, book, plants and candles which Rachel had left for him to find before she took Jodie to the airport. When he did see the shrine, John knelt down beside it and lit the candles; there was a note. He lit a cigarette off one of the fresh white flames and read, 'Dearest John, Now we escape from our bodies. Wait for, Your Rachel.' Trembling, he picked up the book which Rachel had left open at a marked passage; *Addiction To Perfection: The Still Unravished Bride* was a slim red volume. The text was long, and he had to concentrate, but he read as though the passage was a letter from his lover, re-reading each sentence to be sure of its meaning:

Jung believed that religion (religere, to reflect) is one of man's natural instincts, a need that must, therefore, be satisfied. In our world, where the institutionalized sacred is being increasingly profaned, compensation takes over. People begin to treasure their own personal objects and invest them with sacred power. They create their own rituals, but because they don't realise what they are doing they may invoke the wrong god, and be subject to that power whether they like it or not. Again they are trapped into becoming what they worship. If they reject the world as it is, they unconsciously create their own fiction and attempt to project their own 'sacred' world onto the world outside. The resultant collision is increasingly destructive . . .

John leaned back against the wall, watching the pure flames of the candles, so still in the empty room. The face of the plaster Saint – which Saint, John did not know – was upturned and wide-eyed, frozen in devotional piety. Rachel had left other objects – a test-tube filled with vitamin pills, a gold, oily lipstick, a photograph of a teenage boy, standing on the promenade at Brighton, his serious blue eyes narrowed against the glare of the sun. John recognised the face of his lover, feeling the pull of a world which seemed more real than the one that he had left behind, for good.

Nine

Blue, dazzling blue; hot streets in the shadow of the mountains, converging on the Boulevard de la Grotte, where pilgrims sat in the grimy shade, drinking sweetish orange soda before open-fronted shops that were crammed with souvenirs embossed with the figure of a kneeling little girl. The warm air seemed thinner; the bustling economy, wrapped in religion, seemed distant from the business of living. Candles and key-rings, hollow Saints to fill with Holy Water, some no bigger than a child's finger, others the size of a fire-extinguisher – sunlight catching on their ridges of plaster and plastic. Rachel, sitting alone outside a café, at a table with a yellow top, watched the crowds climb down from their stuffy coaches; the deep rumble of engines gave way to the sudden hiss of air brakes.

Rachel was tired; she had been up all night. She leaned back in her chair, her legs stretched out on one another. Sipping Diet Pepsi through a straw, she watched the scene through the reflective acid green lenses of her dark glasses. Endless crowds – groups, couples, families bringing their invalids. Two teenagers guided a wheeled stretcher down the busy street, their dying charge obscured by a pink woollen blanket. Soon, Rachel noticed, they would become entangled in the numerous groups from Spain, who were already assembling with their priests and their embroidered banner before the gates beyond Pont St Michel, where the Avenue des Processions led to the shrine. Rachel remembered working in Lourdes, when she was still a young man; her perverted nature, of course, would have been a desecration – a sin so savage as to lead, in those days, straight to Hell. Feeling the afternoon sun, warm on her arms, Rachel wanted love; more than love, she wanted life.

Jodie was dead – her body had been claimed. She had died in the quiet hotel, before she could visit the shrine. The maid had arrived with the room-service just as Rachel had realised that her friend was never going to wake up again. The maid had assumed that Jodie was asleep. The room was filled with lilies, their cool scent sweetening the dusty air. Rachel's last conversation with Jodie had been about skin care; thin and tired, the dying woman had seemed less substantial than the sheets which covered her. There were two oranges and a peach on a white plate by her elbow. Rachel had sat by the body as the golden afternoon became saffron-coloured dusk. In the evening, listening to car-horns, their short bright notes leaping up to the open windows, she had lifted the telephone to make a start on the bureaucracy of death.

'I've left you some money,' Jodie had said, 'to do whatever you want with . . .'

The most important thing, now, thought Rachel, was that she would be meeting John in Paris, in two days time. She put down her bottle of Pepsi and picked up her bag. The waiter stared at her as she left, his mouth widening into a grin at the sight of her slender figure, her firm breasts and her black leather jacket. He whistled, before turning back to call across the dim interior of his restaurant.

Paris. Along the Rue d'Orsay the wind was keen and blustery, dispelling the memory of southern warmth which Rachel had brought from Lourdes. She had taken a high, big room in a modern hotel on the rue Jacob. The furniture and fittings were grey and angular, the bolster on the wide bed was upholstered in amber and scarlet. On arriving, she had opened the long windows and called John White.

'Now that Jodie's dead . . .' Rachel had rehearsed her phrases on the plane, looking down at the tops of the clouds; she wanted to leave the past behind, and for the changing season to carry John and herself into their new life, whatever that might hold. What else is there? she had thought, lighting her thick, white cigarette and tasting the bitter smoke of the black tobacco; We get older, take stock and find that we can't balance the books – but it's not the end of the world. With one friend, surely, happiness is possible? The rest is self-inflicted. You try to know yourself, to feel alive because of your illnesses, but . . . The thought would not resolve itself. Rachel sipped her orange juice, glad to be sitting on her own. She didn't want to mind so much about the hold of her body on her nature.

'Now that Jodie's dead and I'm in Paris . . .'

John would meet her, the following day, in the cafe on the corner, facing the river. Ragged ribbons of spring cloud would race across the blue sky; they would make their shallow plans.

'Now that we've found each other . . .'

'I'll see you tomorrow,' John had said.

Towards midnight, Rachel climbed off the rumpled sheets of her hotel bed and switched off the soundless television. Long-haired rock and rollers were still screaming at her, flailing with operatic drama into clouds of dry ice and Californian sunsets. She had been asleep since six. She felt strong and happy. She pulled on her old leather jacket, which she loved more than anything else that Jodie had ever given to her; she imagined what farm-boy or mechanic might have bought it new from a small-town shop – she called it Jodie's jacket, because Jodie had found it in Texas, and had known that it was meant for Rachel. In the dim bathroom, she splashed her face with cold water and dabbed some perfume behind her ears. She wanted to go for a walk, to watch the living city. It would be good to let go of the last six months, and to relish her happiness in a foreign city. She found that she couldn't bear the thought of London. There was claustrophobia in the chilly grey streets between White-chapel and Holland Park, Battersea and Highgate; their grid was exposed and joyless, denuded of hope and romance.

Crossing the Seine, Rachel passed under the blackened

imperial arch of the Louvre; she would walk beneath the colonnade of the Rue de Rivoli, on towards . . .

But she thought no more about her journey. Strong, sinewy arms had grabbed at her, and a pale face, with heavy black eyebrows and a swollen lip, was rushing towards her own. Rachel twisted away, but then her legs were kicked from beneath her and a heavy blow knocked the wind out of her lungs. Gasping, she fell to the ground. A car drove by and she tried to scream, but she couldn't hear the sound of her own voice. An elbow hit her hard between her eyes, and she was being dragged into the deep shadows between a high wall and a building-site. The man pushed her down on her back, tugging hard at her leather jacket.

'Take it!' said Rachel, trying to ease the heavy leather off her shoulders, 'Take whatever you want . . .' She looked into the man's face, desperately hoping that she would see some sign in his eyes that she could understand. She could smell his sour breath as he pushed his hands, roughly, under her t-shirt. He twisted her breast and she cried out with pain; her head fell back and she opened her eyes as wide as she could. She saw the blue night sky and a length of rusted razor wire, black and twisted. The man punched Rachel's mouth, splitting her lower lip, and her head struck the corner of a brick. 'This must have been going on for hours,' she thought, as the burning pain above her ear gave way to the warm flow of blood down the side of her face. She tried to jolt her knees, with the last of her strength, as the man thrust his hand down the front of her trousers, twisting his fist between her legs. Rachel's eyes, finally, filled with tears; her assailant's outline was a blur. She did not see his expression change, nor the cruel lock-knife which he pulled from his pocket. He stabbed the transsexual fifteen times before leaving her body beneath the wall. Rachel was dead before he stood up, turned, and kicked out her teeth with the damp toe of his blackened, oily boot.

Consciousness, for a few seconds, was a succession of diminishing perspectives. Then, John remembered Rachel. He looked about the large, bland room. He was in Oporto, in a room in a tall hotel in the centre of town. The room was brown, with square chairs and mirrors. On the long dressing-table, beneath an illuminated mirror, John could see a jumbled still life of his possessions: a half empty bottle of mineral water, two packets of cigarettes, a bottle of tranquilisers, a pack of Prozac, his passport and his keys. He was travelling, he was meant to be meeting his cousin. He couldn't feel despair, because the drugs would not allow despair. He rang for some coffee. 'What time is it?' he asked.

'Thirteen hundred hours . . .'

John put down the phone and walked over to the window. The sky was blue and he could just hear some bells, tolling for some reason a few streets away. Thoughts were struggling to form in his mind, to fall into a pattern which would remind him of the fragments, so at odds with each other, that comprised his life. He knew that he would remember, in a few hours, just what it was he was supposed to be doing. Some gentle truth was close at hand, coyly hiding behind a veil of uncertainty. He picked up the telephone again, and rang the reception desk.

'What time is it?' he asked, once more.

'Thirteen ten . . .'

'And, what city is this?'

He took in the name and sat down on the edge of his bed. Presently, he would light a cigarette. The muffled bells rang out over Oporto, rehearsing the Angelus to a warm white sky, from a tower touched with gold.

Also available in Vintage

Irvine Welsh

THE ACID HOUSE

After his spectacular and controversial opening shot with the cult novel *Trainspotting*, Irvine Welsh follows with an unsettling, shocking, and very funny collection of stories. Using a range of approaches from bitter realism to demented fantasy, Welsh is one of the most uncompromising and original writers around.

'Told with such vigour and alertness, such scathing, unmerciful humour, such compassion and such reserves of linguistic and structural invention that nobody could come away from them without feeling totally exhilarated'
Jonathan Coe, *Sunday Times*

'Another season in hell with Irvine Welsh, and God it's invigorating...The collection as a whole is sick, horrific, occasionally moving and very funny'
New Statesman

'A bruiser with velvet gloves...More that essential reading'
i-D Magazine

VINTAGE

Mary Morrissy

A LAZY EYE

A woman confesses her guilty secret to an obscene caller, a daughter trades with God for her father's life, a family re-enacts an unholy nativity – the characters in *A Lazy Eye* act out a flawed vision of the world. Aggrieved, guilty, betrayed, they seek redemption with disturbing and savage consequences.

'One of the subtlest and most penetrating of the latest generation of Irish writers'
John Banville

'These wonderful short stories... are informed by wit, empathy and quirky imagination... Funny and precisely written'
Sophie Sackville-West, *Evening Standard*

'Morrissy's real interest is in the emotional landscape... the interior life of unease, disappointment, and darkening loneliness... [and she] can create an unforgettable scene'
Irish Times

'Yet another first-class Irish storyteller is among us'
Mike Petty, *Literary Review*

VINTAGE

A SELECTED LIST OF CONTEMPORARY FICTION
AVAILABLE IN VINTAGE

☐	HIGHWAYS AND DANCEHALLS	Diana Atkinson	£5.99
☐	THE FERMATA	Nicholson Baker	£5.99
☐	IN THE KINGDOM OF AIR	Tim Binding	£5.99
☐	THE LONGEST MEMORY	Fred D'Aguiar	£5.99
☐	ARC D'X	Steve Erickson	£5.99
☐	FOREIGN PARTS	Janice Galloway	£5.99
☐	THE FOLDING STAR	Alan Hollinghurst	£5.99
☐	SUNRISE WITH SEA MONSTER	Neil Jordan	£5.99
☐	NOW THAT YOU'RE BACK	A L Kennedy	£5.99
☐	THE UNLOVED	Deborah Levy	£5.99
☐	POMPEY	Jonathan Meades	£5.99
☐	A LAZY EYE	Mary Morrissy	£5.99
☐	MOTHERLAND	Timothy O'Grady	£5.99
☐	FUCKING MARTIN	Dale Peck	£5.99
☐	RADON DAUGHTERS	Iain Sinclair	£5.99
☐	COYOTE	Richard Thornley	£5.99
☐	THE ACID HOUSE	Irvine Welsh	£5.99

- All Vintage books are available through mail order or from your local bookshop.
- Please send cheque/eurocheque/postal order (sterling only), Access, Visa or Mastercard:

☐☐☐☐☐☐☐☐☐☐☐☐☐☐☐☐

Expiry Date: _____ Signature: _____

Please allow 75 pence per book for post and packing U.K.
Overseas customers please allow £1.00 per copy for post and packing.

ALL ORDERS TO:
Vintage Books, Book Service by Post, P.O.Box 29, Douglas, Isle of Man, IM99 1BQ.
Tel: 01624 675137   •   Fax: 01624 670923

NAME: _____

ADDRESS: _____

_____

_____

_____

Please allow 28 days for delivery. Please tick box if you do not
wish to receive any additional information   ☐

Prices and availability subject to change without notice.